P9-DDI-471

Critical Impact

Center Point
Large Print

Also by Linda Hall
and available from Center Point Large Print:

Whisper Lake Trilogy
Storm Warning
On Thin Ice

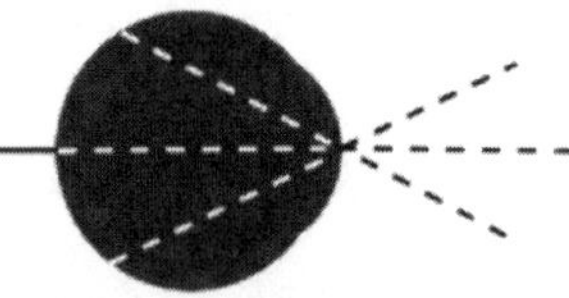

Critical Impact

LINDA HALL

CENTER POINT PUBLISHING
THORNDIKE, MAINE

This Center Point Large Print edition
is published in the year 2010 by arrangement with
Harlequin Books S.A.

This is a work of fiction. Names, characters, places and incidents are either the product of the author's imagination or are used fictitiously, and any resemblance to actual persons, living or dead, business establishments, events or locales is entirely coincidental.

The text of this Large Print edition is unabridged.
In other aspects, this book may vary
from the original edition.
Printed in the United States of America
on permanent paper.
Set in 16-point Times New Roman type.

ISBN: 978-1-60285-936-4

Library of Congress Cataloging-in-Publication Data

Hall, Linda, 1950–
Critical impact / Linda Hall. — Center Point large print ed.
p. cm. — (Whisper Lake series)
Originally published: New York : Steeple Hill, 2010.
ISBN 978-1-60285-936-4 (library binding : alk. paper)
1. Large type books. I. Title. II. Series.
PS3558.A3698C75 2010
813′.54—dc22

2010035111

They that wait upon the Lord shall renew
their strength; they shall mount up with wings as
eagles; they shall run, and not be weary;
and they shall walk, and not faint.

—*Isaiah* 40:31

ONE

When Anna Barker reached out to open the heavy wooden door of City Hall, she was hurled backward in a blinding flash and a crush of ear-rupturing noise.

It happened fast. One second she was carrying her grande latte, her large stage makeup bag and several books of photographs, and trying to avoid the leering glances of the mayor, the next she was flattened on the ground beside the building, nose pressed into the grass.

She lay there, stunned. She didn't move, couldn't. At first nothing hurt. And then everything did. Her left arm was sprawled next to her body and her other hand was up next to her face. She felt a burning on her neck and shoulders. She raised her hand to check the liquid. Blood? No. Hot coffee. She could tell by the smell of it. She had spilled her coffee.

A spasm of coughs rattled her chest. She spat out some dirt. That small exertion sent coils of pain through her core. She took tiny breaths—deep ones hurt—and tried to steady herself. Everything around her was noiseless, still and surreal. It was like she had been cast into some deep, suffocating cave. She opened her eyes and was filled with a horrid sense of terror. She couldn't hear herself cough. She felt, but didn't hear, the groans that welled up from inside her. She blinked and the movement hurt. She was confused. Where was she? What had just happened?

Gingerly, she tried to take stock of her surroundings. She was lying on a patch of lawn in front of the City Hall building in Shawnigan, Maine. Anna's brain told her to rise, to get up, to run, but the rest of her body would not respond.

She tried to remember. First, she had been walking up toward City Hall, then the mayor had come, accosted her and finally gone in ahead of her. Next thing she knew there had been that thunderous sound and bursting light. And she had ended up here. Could it have been the bomb? It had to be the bomb. But no, the bomb for the mock disaster wasn't scheduled until tomorrow. And it wasn't going to be a real bomb, anyway. Just smoke and noise. A simulation.

Maybe something about the bomb had gone terribly wrong.

Her throat was raw and she forced herself to move her head, cast a backward glance toward the building she had almost entered. All she saw was bricks, gray stones and rubble. Where was Mayor Johnny Seeley? He'd been just ahead of her. And earlier two of her esthetics students, Hilary and Claire, had gone inside. She had come early to talk with Hilary. Were they somewhere in all that rubble? Were they okay?

Her eyes felt scratchy. Why was everything blurry? She guessed that her contact lenses must have come out in the blast. She raised her head.

People were running toward her, climbing over shattered pieces of the fountain that used to be in front of City Hall. Splashing through the water that gushed from its broken facade. Through hazy eyes she saw the lights of police cars. She shifted her gaze and saw the back of a broad-shouldered man in a red shirt leaning over and gesturing to a woman. Her hand was raised and she appeared to be holding something. Were they looking at her? She wished she could see better.

Was that . . . ? No. It couldn't be! Was it Peter? Had he followed her to Maine? No! She squinted and tried to clear her gritty vision. She turned away, lest he see her, come for her . . .

She needed to get up, scramble away from this place. Away from him. But she couldn't move her body.

Help me! God, help me!

In the opposite direction from where Peter was, she saw a man running toward her, his hands cupped around his mouth. He was calling to her, but she couldn't hear a thing.

She looked up in time to see a wall of stone plummet toward her, gray rocks tumbling into each other as they fell, surrounding her, entombing her.

• • •

Stu McCabe had been standing beside the hospital auxiliary tent and squirting a line of mustard on his free hot dog when he heard the explosion. Ahead of him, he watched in horror as the entire front of City Hall seemed to fold in on itself.

An earthquake? No. He would have felt an earthquake. People were screaming now and running in all directions. He ran toward the building because he had seen a woman fall. He needed to get to her!

Anna regained consciousness slowly. When she finally did, all she felt was pain. It seared white-hot down her arm and it intensified in her wrist. She was lying flat, the right side of her face pressed against something hard and jagged. Her right arm was pinned.

She groaned, heard nothing but the pounding of her heart and a roaring in her ears. When she opened her eyes, she saw only blurred darkness. She tried to move her head a bit to see where she was, but she trembled with pain, and shook with cold and shock.

She knew she was under rocks and debris, yet somehow, the cascading stones hadn't crushed her. Her torso was being protected by something flat and square. A door? Maybe. She worried that if she moved, even slightly, it would come down and crush her completely. Already she was finding it difficult to breathe. She had to concentrate. *Breathe in. Breathe out. In. Out.*

She closed her eyes against the pain and inhaled the acrid smell of fire and sulfur. She coughed, and each raspy cough sent hot pain into her chest and across her arm and into her wrist. She felt pain right down to the tips of her fingers. She tried making any small sound she could, but didn't know if she was heard by anyone. She heard only the roaring in her ears.

The thought came to her that she might actually die in here. This was what it was like to be buried alive. She coughed again and finally she prayed.

God, help me to get out of here, but if not, help me not to be afraid.

She prayed this over and over and over. Slowly, she realized that despite everything, she was somehow still breathing. Clean air was getting to her from somewhere. She felt a tiny waft of cool air on the very top of her head. With great effort she moved her eyes to where she could almost see the pinhole between the rocks and rubble. It might be enough to survive. She tried to ignore the grinding pain in her right arm as she turned her face, moved it toward that gap in the rubble and gulped in pure air.

Quietly, she began to sing the new hymn she had learned last week in church about God's protection.

She sensed movement above her and prayed that

whatever it was it wouldn't send the piece of flat rock into her chest.

Time passed, but she couldn't tell how much. She kept breathing, and kept thanking God for the gift of air. She drifted in and out of consciousness.

She came awake again when she felt a warm touch on the fingers of her left hand. She opened her eyes and stared up into the face of a man. He was talking to her, but she couldn't hear him. She closed her eyes.

Slowly, one by one, pieces of rock and debris were moved away from her head and then her body. The pain was unbearable when they moved the slab away from her wrist. Tears filled her eyes. She moaned and she blacked out again from the pain.

Every once in a while she would open her eyes. And when she did, she looked up into the man's face. His smile gave her hope.

The trapped woman looked so helpless. When all of the rubble had been painstakingly removed piece by piece, he gently reached down and cupped his hands around her dusty head.

He recognized her. He didn't know her, had never officially met her, but she'd been to some of the planning meetings. If he was not mistaken, she was the one in charge of making the victims of the mock disaster look as real as possible. He winced when one of the EMTs moved the piece of cement from on top of her right hand. It looked crushed. No wonder she was drifting in and out of consciousness with the pain.

Two EMTs placed the stretcher as close as they could to her twisted form. The main thing was to keep her back and neck immobilized. Her eyes were closed, but she was saying something. He bent his head close to her face.

"Yes?" he said.

She wasn't talking. She was humming something.

"You're going to be all right," he told her as he smoothed bits of dust and debris from her hair.

She opened her eyes and looked up at him. He couldn't help himself. He smiled down at her. As they carried her stretcher past the crowds of people who were beginning to mill about, he kept his eyes on her face. And as he did so, he thought about another woman, a woman he was not able to save from another bomb in another time and place.

He vowed that this time would be different.

When next she opened her eyes, she knew she was in the back of a fast-moving ambulance by the equipment that surrounded her. Every rut, every bump in the road sent shivers of pain down her arm.

The man was still here, the man whose face she had looked into when she was lying in the rubble.

She couldn't hear him, but she looked at his mouth and was able to read his lips. He was saying, "Don't worry. You're safe now. You're safe now."

But as she closed her eyes she wondered if she would ever be safe if Peter was back.

TWO

Anna opened her eyes. She was on her back in a single bed, blanketed to her neck in white. She was in a shadowy, dim hospital room.

She looked down at the bed. Her right arm was encased in a white plaster cast that went from her shoulder clear down to the ends of her fingers. Her arm was also hooked into a kind of contraption that held it completely immobile and slightly away from her body. Her left hand lay next to her, but a clear tube snaked from her inner wrist to an IV bag on a stand beside her. Just in front of the IV stand there was a movable bedside table with two bouquets—some stemmed flowers in a vase plus an orange potted mum.

Her gaze went back to her right arm. She was an esthetician. She was right-handed. Before this happened, she'd been working on Whisper Lake County's mock disaster drill. As head of makeup, it was her job to make the fake wounds on the pretend victims look realistic.

The mock disaster was going to test the readiness of Whisper Lake County's fire and police departments, EMTs, hospital and search-and-rescue team. Was it still going to happen? Had it happened?

A movement to her left caught her attention. A man was standing beside her window, silhouetted by the streetlight outside. His back was to her. Hands in his pockets, he peered out at the night, seemingly deep in thought. For one horrible moment she thought it was Peter, and she shrugged away from the form and down into her blankets.

Her slight movement must have caught his attention, because he turned to her. It was a man she didn't know—yet she somehow did. And when he smiled at her, she remembered. This was the face she had looked up at, the man who had found her, rescued her and smoothed her hair away from her face as he rode with her in the ambulance to the hospital.

His face broke out in a grin and he came toward her. He was saying something to her, but it was muzzy in her ears.

He came closer. "Hello," he said.

She tried to say something, but her voice was hoarse and crackly. She cleared her throat. "Hi," she said.

"Miss Barker, I'm Deputy Stu McCabe, and this is Deputy Liz Corcoran," he said, gesturing toward a young lady who was now getting out of the chair by the door. Anna noticed for the first time that a woman was in her room. She was tall and long-limbed.

"How are you doing?" he asked her. She squinted up at him. His face was slightly blurry around the edges. Her contact lenses were gone, so nothing was really too clear. He was tall and was wearing a brown sweater. His hair was light and, from what she could see, cut short, like a military hairstyle.

"I don't know," she answered. That was the truth. Right now she felt numb. She had so many questions, some that she was afraid to ask. Had it been a bomb? A gas explosion? An earthquake?

There was a deep, dull pain in her right arm. Her face hurt, and so did her left wrist where the IV was attached.

He bent toward her. "When you're up to it, we'd like to ask you a few questions."

She nodded. That's the reason he was here. He was a police officer with questions. He had picked her up, held her closely and talked kindly to her on the way to the hospital simply because it was his job. It made her feel let down in a way she couldn't define.

"Okay." Her voice broke. "But can you first tell me what happened?"

His face darkened. "A bomb." He said it simply.

A bomb! Her eyes went wide. "Why? What . . . ?"

The woman named Liz came and stood beside Deputy McCabe and said, "We don't know. We're still trying to piece things together."

"What time is it?" Anna suddenly asked. When had this all occurred? She looked helplessly at her right hand where she normally wore a silver watch.

"Around 9:00 p.m.," Deputy McCabe said.

"Wow," she said, opening her eyes wide. "I've been here the whole time?"

"They just brought you to your room. You were in surgery for quite a while. Your family is in the hall. Your mother is here."

"My mother's here?" Anna was finding it difficult to tear her eyes away from this man.

"We met your mother, Catherine, and your aunt, Lois."

"Good. Um . . ." She was desperate for facts. "So it was a bomb? Did it have something to do with the mock disaster?" Her voice echoed in her own head as she spoke, but at least her hearing was getting better. "Did it go off accidentally?"

"No," Deputy McCabe said. "It didn't. It wasn't supposed to be a real bomb. Just smoke bombs."

"Pretty coincidental timing, though," Liz said.

"Was it . . . terrorists?" She shifted slightly in her bed, but quickly came to the conclusion that any movement, no matter how slight, caused pain.

"Again, we don't know," he said.

Liz added, "At this point we're looking at every possibility."

"What about the others?" she asked. "Two of my students went in ahead of me." Her head was spinning. Hilary had been inside City Hall and Claire, too. Plus, the mayor.

Deputy McCabe paused, took a breath. "Hilary Jonas and Claire Sweeney have been positively identified. They died this morning in the blast. I'm so very sorry, Anna."

Anna swallowed several times. Tears welled up in her eyes. How could they be dead? She had been with those girls just yesterday. "What about Mayor Seeley? He also went into the building just ahead of me."

"They rushed him by air ambulance to Portland. We haven't heard anything yet."

She tried to lift her left hand to wipe her eyes, but it was tethered to the IV pole. She felt helpless. Deputy McCabe took a tissue from the box beside her and gently wiped her eyes. The gentle act made her tear up even more. She fought to regain her composure.

"Who would do this?" she gasped.

"That's what we're trying to find out," Liz said. "That's why we'd like to ask you some questions before your family comes back in."

"Okay," she said. "I don't know how I can be of help, but okay."

Deputy McCabe began asking questions. As best she could, Anna told them everything she saw, or didn't see just before entering the building. They asked the same questions in many different ways, and she answered until her voice was hoarse and she couldn't think. She hadn't paid too much attention to what had been going on around her. Her mind had been on her lesson plan. There was still so much she had needed to get done before the mock disaster. She told them this, too.

When Deputy Corcoran asked her if she had received any threats lately, Anna paused. Deputy McCabe seemed to notice this pause and looked at her expectantly. Did Peter count? Should she tell them about Peter? But Peter was her own business.

She'd never said goodbye to Peter. Was that it? Some weird and awful act of revenge? Peter had lied to her. He'd told her he was a Christian. He'd told her she was special to him. All lies. And on that last date, when he slammed her up against the brick fireplace of his mansion, she thought he intended to rape her. But even if he wasn't going to rape her, she knew she had to leave. That's all he wanted from her. That's why he lied. He didn't want her for herself. She knew she had to get away from him. She had hit him hard in the chest and loudly said, "No!" until he lost his grip on her shoulders and she shoved him away, then ran.

The following day she left California.

She had been back in Maine a month when she received his e-mail.

The next time we meet, you'll regret it. I will be back.

Did that constitute a threat?

She took a deep breath and told them about Peter. If he had done this, he deserved to get caught. She gave them Peter's contact information.

Deputy McCabe wrote it all down.

She heard voices in the hall.

"Anna! Oh, Anna!" She turned toward the door. Her mother, Catherine, was there, along with her mother's sister, Lois. "Can we see her now?" her mother asked.

"Yes," Deputy McCabe said. "Come in."

Anna gave them a weak, "Hi!"

Her mother rushed toward her. "You gave us quite a scare. You were in surgery so long."

"No one would tell us a thing," her aunt, Lois, added.

Anna didn't see the two officers leave, but the next time she looked up, they were gone.

Her mother kissed her cheek and whispered, "I'm so glad you're okay. We've all been praying so hard. I put you on the prayer line at our church, and Lois had you on the prayer line at her church."

"Thank you." But here is where Anna had her first inkling of a serious question. Two young women had died. Was she alive because she had more people praying for her? And did they die because no one prayed for them? Why had God protected her, but left Hilary and Claire to die?

"We were so worried about you," Aunt Lois added. "It's been all over the news. Everywhere!"

Anna nodded.

"Are you in pain, dear?" her mother asked. "Should I call the nurse? The doctor's on her way. I know she wants to talk to you."

"That's good." Anna tried not to wince.

Lois said, "We'll get the nurse. I can tell by your face that you need something for the pain."

Anna's head felt muzzy. All she wanted to do was sleep.

"We won't stay long," her mother said, smoothing her bangs away from her face. "We'll be back in the morning. I'll bring you your Bible and some magazines and books. Is there anything else you'd like?"

"Can you bring me my glasses?" she asked. "They're in my top dresser drawer in the cottage I'm renting. I lost my contact lenses somewhere."

"Certainly, dear," her mother said, writing all this down on a piece of paper.

"I'm in the cottage closest to the water."

"I know, dear."

"You can get the key from Bette. I don't know where my purse is."

"Bette has already phoned us," Lois said. "She sends you a hug."

When Anna had moved back home to Whisper Lake Crossing in such a hurry, her mother had tried to persuade her to move into the cottage that she and her sister shared. Anna declined. She wanted—needed—her own place.

For her entire life, all Anna had ever wanted to do was to fix people's hair and play with makeup. It was a fascination that sometimes furrowed her mother's brows. What kind of career was esthetics for a nice Christian girl? Yet, when it became evident that Anna would not be swayed in her career goal, her mother reluctantly decided to support her. Anna breezed through Shawnigan Community College and was hired at a local spa. When a teaching job opened up, Anna applied for it and was accepted. She enjoyed teaching, but knew that what she really wanted to do was stage makeup.

Hollywood had beckoned. Maybe if she moved to California she could get a job doing makeup for movies. She packed up and moved. She'd apply for a job once she got there. She had never done anything quite so reckless before.

But what she didn't fully understand was the hierarchy in movie land. It made no difference what you knew, it was who you knew. She worked at networking. She met Peter and he promised her things. He said he could get her a job. He did.

But then she owed him.

Six months ago she came home to Maine without saying goodbye to anyone. Her mother knew what had happened, but her mother was the only one.

Anna was currently renting a cottage in a resort called Flower Cottage, which was only a few minutes' walk along the lakefront from her mother's cottage.

"And when you get out of the hospital, whenever that may be, you'll be staying with us," her mother added. "The new windows came today. You'll stay in the parlor. We've already been talking about that."

Anna smiled up at her mother and her aunt—her only family. The sisters were only a year apart in age, and no one would mistake them for being anything but sisters. Yet their personalities were like the moon and the sun. Her mother was soft-spoken and introverted while Lois was opinionated, outspoken and extroverted. When Lois's husband died and Catherine invited her to come live in the cottage, Anna worried that Lois would take advantage of her mother, yet Catherine seemed to be holding her own. And for this, Anna was glad.

But what would it be like to add a third person to the mix? She closed her eyes. Maybe she wouldn't have to find out. Maybe she could go home to her little rented cottage by the lake.

But without the use of her right hand for a while, she guessed she would have no choice but to stay at her mother's.

"I hate to break up this party," a nurse said. "But we need to get Anna ready for the night. And it's way past visiting hours. The doctor will be here in a few minutes."

The sisters kissed her good-night and left.

"I'm Sara," the nurse said when her visitors left. "I'm your night nurse. If there's anything you need, please call me. I'll clip the button right here beside your left hand. Is that okay?"

“Thank you.”

The doctor was an orthopedic surgeon named Dr. Neale, who told her that she was indeed lucky that her right hand hadn’t been entirely crushed. It had been touch and go for a while, the doctor explained.

Anna nodded.

The doctor went on. It didn’t look as if crucial nerves had been damaged, and they were doing everything they could to save her hand. The cast and splints had been configured to provide the least mobility now at this critical stage.

Save her hand? Anna blinked. She was told that her wrist and hand would require further surgeries, plus lots of physiotherapy. The doctor concluded by saying that her muffled hearing as a result of the blast should be temporary. Anna nodded, took the proffered pain pills and drifted off to sleep.

Anna woke up. It was dark. A doctor in green scrubs, a surgical mask and a bonnet was standing at the foot of her bed and holding a pillow. Anna squinted. Were they taking her for more surgery? She would be glad when her mother brought her glasses tomorrow. What did this doctor want? More blood? A check of her vitals? To change the IV?

The person with the pillow simply stood there and looked at her without moving.

Finally, Anna said, “Hello?” Her middle-of-the-night voice was feeble and hoarse.

No response.

Anna said it more loudly. "Yes?"

The person in the green scrubs moved to the side of her bed. Then the doctor bent down close to Anna, and with one quick movement plunged the pillow into Anna's face.

Anna writhed and whipped her head from side to side, trying to break free. It was as if she were in the cave of rubble all over again.

She remembered suddenly about the nurse call button. Sara had said she had clipped it beside her left hand. Was it still there? She grasped for it, somehow found it, and pressed it over and over again.

She felt she was going to lose consciousness when she dimly heard from the PA beside her, "Anna—it's Nurse Sara, I'm on my way."

The pillow and the doctor in green had vanished by the time Sara arrived.

"Someone tried to smother me!" Anna blurted out, tears running down her cheeks.

"What!"

"Someone was just in here. All in green. And he tried to smother me with a pillow."

Sara went out into the hallway. A few moments later she was back again. "I didn't see anyone in the hallway, Anna. There's no one else here tonight. It's a very quiet night."

"But there was someone. It was a doctor and he put a pillow on my face." Anna couldn't breathe.

"He was wearing all dark green and a mask, like a surgeon."

Sara sat down beside her and put her hand on Anna's left arm. "Anna, there's no one here. One of the side effects of the amount and type of pain medications you're on is the feeling of being smothered sometimes. I'll talk to the doctor about it in the morning. In the meantime, would you like me to sit with you for a while?"

"I would. Thank you."

With tears stinging her eyes, Anna finally drifted off to sleep. Had someone really been here? Or had it been a dream of the worst kind?

THREE

"Your best guess—you guys think what happened at City Hall was an act of terrorism?" Stu poured himself a cup of coffee. He was pretty sure the coffee in the pot had been sitting on the counter in the Whisper Lake Crossing Sheriff's Office for at least five hours. But since yesterday, Deputy Stu McCabe, Sheriff Alec Black and Deputy Liz Corcoran had been too busy to even rinse out the coffeepot after batches. To make it more palatable, Stu stirred in two spoonfuls of powdered creamer and three spoonfuls of sugar. He stood beside the window and stirred his coffee while he looked at the TV van parked outside.

"I do," Liz answered, looking up at him. "Anybody who sets off a bomb is a terrorist. Plain and simple." According to Liz, who had recently moved to Whisper Lake Crossing, all crimes had to do with terrorists, gangs or drugs. "It can't be any of these weirdos on the anonymous tip line," she said, holding up the phone. "I just talked to a guy. Says he's the bomber. Says he's also single-handedly responsible for assassinating JFK."

"I hope you took down his name." Alec looked up from his desk and over the tops of his skinny reading glasses. "Anybody who calls in is a potential suspect."

"I know, I know . . ." She went back to the

phone, holding up a yellow pad half-full of notes, numbers and details.

As any police officer knew, a tip line tended to bring out all the crazies from the woodwork, yet each tip had to be written down, analyzed and followed up on.

Alec and Stu and Liz had been at this for twenty-four hours and all they seemed to have succeeded in doing was getting the national media here in full force. Even now, a national news van, complete with a satellite dish, was parked out front. A well-dressed anchorwoman holding a microphone was being filmed, and the Whisper Lake Crossing Sheriff's Department was the backdrop for this scene.

Most of the media action was centered ten miles south at Shawnigan, Maine, where forensics and bomb specialists were still sifting through the rubble. But since Anna Barker and Mayor Johnny Seeley were from Whisper Lake Crossing, this town was also prominently in the news.

The mock disaster was to have been for the entire county of Whisper Lake, which included the communities of Whisper Lake Crossing, Shawnigan at the southern tip and DeLorme in the north.

Of course, the disaster drill had been canceled due to the real disaster, something that the media was finding both ironic and newsworthy.

Stu decided that he'd had enough of a walking-around break. Time to get back to work. All morning he'd been trying to track down the elusive Peter Remington, former boyfriend of Anna Barker.

Anna had left California, "escaped," she told him, from an ex-boyfriend who had "threatened" her. She'd given him Peter's contact information, but the e-mails bounced. Stu had left countless messages to no avail.

Alec looked at Stu. "Any more on Anna Barker? You going to see her today?"

"Planning to. After I make a few more calls here."

Because Stu had been the one who had found and rescued Anna, Alec had decided that he should be the one to keep in contact with her. This was fine with Stu. She was the pretty, dark-haired woman with the sad face who mostly kept to herself. She always looked so perfectly polished and therefore out of his league.

When the explosion happened and he'd seen a woman fall, he'd had no idea it was her. His adrenaline had kicked in and he ran to help. It had done something to his heart when he discovered it was her underneath that rubble.

But even with the scratches and gashes on her face, she looked beautiful to him. He had been saddened to learn that she'd been so hurt by a jerk in California. A jerk he was now having no luck tracking down.

He searched the guy's name on the Internet and came up with accolades on his great special effects. The company he worked for had even been nominated for an Academy Award once. Stu had run the guy's name through the police databases they had access to and come up with no information. He had no criminal record.

Stu sat down and called the studio in California where Peter worked.

"No," a gruff female voice answered. "Peter Remington isn't here. Who wants to know?"

Stu introduced himself.

"The police? *Maine?* He in some kind of trouble?"

"We need to talk with him about something."

"All I can say is if you find him, you can tell him to get his sorry self back here. He's the only one who knows the correct bomb sequence and we can't produce this scene without him. He's holding up editing. He's holding up production."

Stu straightened in his chair. "What do you mean by bomb sequence?"

"For the movie. He's the one who's putting it all together."

"So Peter Remington knows a lot about bombs?"

"He's the best."

"And you don't know where he is?" Stu was taking rapid notes.

"Nope. Not a clue."

Stu thanked the woman and got her to promise to call him if Peter did show up.

Well, well, thought Stu.

He was finishing up his notes when a movement in the doorway caught his attention. A tall, hollow-cheeked young man with purple spiky hair and thick eyebrows stood there holding a black art portfolio. Since Stu's desk was closest to the door, he got up. "Can I help you? Something you need?"

The man shifted from foot to foot, clearly nervous. He wore shiny black boots, which came clear to his knees.

"Maybe," he said. "I found something. Don't know if it's important or not."

"What is it pertaining to?" Stu asked him.

"It's about the bombing at the Shawnigan City Hall yesterday."

Stu invited him over to have a seat at his desk. The young man did and coiled his long legs around the front of the chair, leaning in toward Stu. His patent-leather boots squeaked.

"My name's Rodney Malini. I'm a friend of Anna's."

Rodney laid the portfolio down on the desk and proceeded to pull out sheets of papers.

"Well, actually, I'm one of Anna's students. I am . . . was . . . good friends with Hilary and Claire. Our class was pretty tight. Anna's a great teacher. And last night . . . well, last night I was just so upset over everything that I couldn't even think straight. Couldn't sleep at all. So I got looking around the Internet. I started reading Hilary's blog. Don't know if it means anything but I thought the police should see it, maybe."

Scanning the top of the sheets, Stu asked, "You live in Shawnigan?"

The young man nodded.

"You drove all the way up here instead of going to the police station down there?"

"Shawnigan's a crazy place. TV cameras everywhere, man. I don't like the limelight so much."

Stu stared at him. He had certainly dressed oddly for someone who didn't like the limelight so much. "There's a television crew outside here now," Stu said.

"I managed to avoid them. But this is what I wanted to show you."

Stu picked up the top sheet. Rodney pointed. "It's that line there I thought you should read."

I know she wants to hurt me, and even get me out of the way.

"And here's another one."

She threatened me again today.

There were a couple more printed pages like this. With entries like, *She's stalking me. I can't take it,* all highlighted by Rodney's yellow marker.

Stu looked at him and then back at the blog

sheets. "You said you were good friends with Hilary. Do you know who she was writing about?"

Rodney shook his head. "We, all of us were tight, but Hilary—she was a little different. Quiet. Didn't talk much. I don't know. I have no idea, in fact. I talked with some of the others, and no one knows. She kept to herself a lot. Hilary also kept a poetry blog. She also wrote poetry. She's one of those people who writes everything down." His eyes swam with tears when he realized the verb tense mistake he had made. He corrected himself, "She wrote everything down. I'm going to see Anna," he said suddenly. "Do you know if she can have visitors?"

"I'm pretty sure she can," Stu said. "But check with the hospital."

Before Rodney left, Stu wrote down the Web site address and took Rodney's contact information. Stu handed him a business card and said, "Anything else you remember, please call me. I wrote my cell number on the back of the card."

Rodney left.

So *Hilary* could have been the target?

Anna decided not to tell anyone about almost being smothered the previous night—not her mother, nor her aunt, nor Deputy McCabe. Sara and Daphne, the day nurse, had convinced her that the pain medication had made her feel smothered.

In the morning, Daphne gently removed the bandages on Anna's face, washed the wounds, as well as the rest of her face, and re-bandaged them.

"It's healing nicely," Daphne said.

"That's good. In some ways my face hurts more than my arm."

"That sometimes happens." The nurse paused. "I heard you had an episode last night."

Anna nodded. *An episode.* "It felt so real," she said.

"That's morphine for you. It relieves serious pain, but we always have to watch the side effects." Daphne gave her a rundown of the side effects, everything from nausea to a feeling of being smothered.

They were probably right, after all. Anna had never taken such powerful pills in her life. She had never even spent any time in the hospital—until now.

Daphne took her temperature, her blood pressure, checked on a few more things and gave her a tiny white paper cup of pills and a glass of water.

"What are these?"

"Antibiotics. We're holding off on the pain pills until the doctor gets here. She's just down the hall. She'll be by in a minute. And then," Daphne said, "you have someone waiting to see you."

The handsome police officer? she wondered. She hoped.

When the doctor came in, all crisp and white and holding a chart, she said, "I hear morphine isn't working so well for you, is it?"

"I guess not," Anna said.

"We have a whole arsenal of pain medication at our disposal. If one doesn't work, there are always others."

"Good."

When the doctor left and her visitor arrived, she was charmed to see that it was Rodney. She loved her oddball student, with his flashy clothes and dyed hair, who wanted to design for stage makeup. He was talented and dedicated, her only male student in her class of females.

He came over and pulled up the chair next to her bed.

"It's nice of you to drive all the way up here to see me, Rodney," she said.

"I had to come up to give something to the police," he said.

Anna looked at him.

"It was about Hilary." He told her that he'd found an online blog Hilary had written, indicating that she was being stalked.

This brought new tears to Anna's eyes. She had never connected with the girl, although she had tried many times. On the morning of Hilary's death, Anna had intended to have a private conference with the girl, who was in danger of failing the course. And then Johnny Seeley, who, as mayor of Whisper Lake Crossing, shouldn't even have been in Shawnigan in the first place, slowed her down.

The delay saved her life. And yet Hilary and Claire were gone. None of it made sense.

She stifled a sob when she thought about that. Rodney put his hand on her left arm and wept like a baby. They both did.

"I can't believe it," he said over and over. "I was talking to Claire just yesterday morning. Oh, Anna," he said. "What are we going to do? I don't think I'll be able to even go to their funerals. I'm afraid I would just turn into a puddle and melt right there in the church."

"You'll be okay, Rodney. We all will. I'll be praying for you."

"Oh, can you pray right now?"

Anna did.

When he left, Nurse Daphne came in with another pill for her to take, one eyebrow raised at the departing Rodney. "Who was that?" she asked.

"A good friend of mine."

When Deputy McCabe came in a few minutes later he presented her with a bouquet of bright, saucer-size mums.

"Thank you," she said. "They're beautiful."

He studied them. "They are kind of nice. They're from Bette. She heard what happened and wanted you to have a couple of her prize mums."

So they were from Bette and not from him. She

didn't know why she felt such a sudden disappointment. After all, why should she expect flowers from the police officer who was questioning her?

"I'm living at Bette's resort now," she said. "For the time being, until I find a place of my own. It's beautiful there. Bette is such a fine gardener. I've been savoring the fall colors in her many gardens."

"Actually, I think it's her son, Ralph, who does most of the gardening."

She nodded. "I've seen him out there. It's been such a peaceful place for me to live. It's been a good place for me to get some rest and get my act together." Yesterday, during the questioning, she had told them so much about Peter. Her life was an open book as far as the police were concerned. It made her feel vulnerable in front of this man about whom she knew nothing. He could be engaged for all she knew. And why should she be thinking about him in this way?

Deputy McCabe sat in the chair recently vacated by Rodney. "How are you, Anna? How do you feel this morning?"

It really seemed like he was concerned for her, the way he was looking at her. She felt herself blushing under his intense gaze. She looked over at her right arm in its awkward and heavy cast. "I'm going to run a marathon this afternoon, Deputy McCabe. You want to come?"

He grinned. "Why don't you call me Stu."

"Okay, Stu."

"I also brought some of your things from the bomb site."

Her eyes watered when she looked at the ash-covered handbag filled with stage makeup. The photograph book was charred and the cover was bent. She looked through the bag. "My wallet's not here," she said.

"That's all we found at the site," said Stu. "Are you up for any more questions?"

"Okay. But where's my wallet?"

"I'm not sure," he said. "If they find it, I'll let you know. They're still working out there in the site. They haven't recovered there yet. I'll bring it to you when they find it."

"Thank you. They just gave me another pain pill. So I may fall asleep at any moment, or say weird things. I'm just warning you."

"Duly noted," he said with a smile. "I would like you to go over again everything you saw."

"Again?"

"Can you remember anything else? Any more details? Anything you saw or heard?"

She shook her head. "Since the blast momentarily muffled my hearing, no, I didn't hear anything."

He took out some sheets of paper from a folder. "One of your students, a young man named Rodney Malini, came to see me this morning."

Anna nodded. "He was just in here. He told me about Hilary's online blog."

Stu laid the printouts from the blog on the tray table beside her and pushed it toward her. She picked the top one up with her left hand. Fortunately, she only needed her glasses for distance vision. She could read okay without them. And what she read disturbed her.

Stu asked, "Do you have any idea who she was writing about?"

Anna said she didn't. She picked up another page and read. And then another and another. Finally, she looked up at Stu. "So you think the bombing was aimed at Hilary? That someone wanted to kill *her?*" She knew Hilary had seemed unhappy, but was it this serious?

"Did all of your students get along?" Stu asked.

"They seemed to. I'm not a part of their private lives, but I didn't seem to notice any jealousy or any rivalries, other than the fact that Hilary seemed quieter than the rest, more moody somehow."

"When did you first notice this?"

Anna thought about that. "Right from the beginning, I think. But I've only been with this group since I came home from California. Have you spoken to her family?"

"Not yet. Deputy Liz will be going there today." He paused. "I'd like to talk to you about something else, too. About Peter."

Hearing Peter's name caused her to swallow and blink rapidly.

He pulled his chair even closer to her. "I've been trying to reach him and I can't. He's not answering any of his phones."

"He never does. He monitors all his calls, and only calls back people he wants to talk to."

"He hasn't gone to work. I called the studio."

The mention of the studio caused Anna to swallow. That's the place where she had worked, too.

Stu said, "He seems to be gone and no one knows where he is. I was just wondering if you knew where he might be. He's supposed to be working on a movie and he's not there."

She said, "It's not unusual for him to take off and fly under the radar for a while. He was always pulling stunts like this. . . ." Anna's voice trailed off and she looked down at her left hand. It was pale, the same color as the sheet.

Stu said, "I'm sorry he hurt you so much."

Anna nodded.

"We were only together for a couple of months. I met him at a party. When I told him I wanted to do movie makeup, he recommended me for a job and the next day I got a call. It went from there." She shook her head, all these thoughts tumbling together in her memory. "I enjoyed what I did, but the life there . . ." She paused. "I never felt like I fit in."

"What about his bomb-making?"

"Peter did special effects. In movies. Not for real."

"He never made real bombs?"

"He worked with explosives, but it's mostly smoke and mirrors in movies, Stu."

Stu nodded and wrote something down. She closed her eyes and drifted off for a mere second. The pain medication and the antibiotic were beginning to take effect. She blinked, her eyes open. "I'm sorry," she said. "I seem to be fading."

He stood up. "If Peter gets in touch with you, or if you remember anything else, or if anything jumps into your mind, be sure to call me right away." He left another business card on her tray.

"Stu?" she called.

He turned. "Yes?"

"Will you keep me in the loop, let me know what's going on?"

He said he would and left.

And as she watched him go, it seemed to her that there was something that happened right before the blast, something that she should be remembering.

And that it had something to do with Peter. Or was she just thinking about Peter because Stu had brought him up?

FOUR

Stu didn't need to be distracted by a woman, especially one who was involved in a police investigation. But this was exactly what was happening. He pulled out of the hospital parking lot, unable to get Anna's face out of his mind.

This reaction surprised him. After his wife died six years ago, he never thought that he would be interested in any woman again. He hardly knew Anna. Yet, there was something about her that intrigued him.

He shook his head. He couldn't allow his emotions to get away from him. He thought he would never get over the loss of his wife, and he couldn't risk losing another. Therefore, he needed to stop all thoughts of Anna Barker before they began.

He frowned as he headed out onto the highway that led down to Shawnigan. He turned on the radio in the patrol car. Maybe that would get his mind off Anna and back onto the case.

The highway was pretty empty on this golden autumn day. The only other car was a silver one, which glinted behind him. It passed him by when he turned right onto the narrow road that led to the place where he was meeting Liz.

The paved road became narrower, and then turned into a crunchy gravel, one-lane path with overgrown brush on either side. The patrol car scraped its way through and Stu rolled down the window, letting in the warm air. It wasn't too long up the road before he heard the gunfire.

The rutted path opened up to a wide, flat area dotted with a few faded clapboard buildings, wooden stands and picnic tables. The shooting range was set against the natural backdrop of a dirt and gravel cliff face.

Liz was the only person there and intent as she was, it didn't appear that she had heard him drive up. He stopped the car and watched her for a few minutes. Without making a sound, he got out of the car and leaned against it. He knew better than to call out to her when Liz was concentrating on her shot.

Without turning around she said, "I know you're there, McCabe." She always called him by his last name.

"Just watching," he said.

Carefully, slowly, she pulled the trigger twice. The blast was thunderous in the canyon. He had no doubt that her shots had landed right in the center of the target. He walked down with her and sure enough, the shots had.

While Stu was talking with Anna, Liz elected to spend the time at the shooting range, so Stu had dropped her here earlier.

"I saw Anna," he said, walking back from the target area. "She has no idea who Hilary was writing about."

"Somehow I didn't figure she would," Liz said. "Personally, I think we're barking up the wrong tree with Anna Barker."

"You might be right," Stu said, feeling strangely let down. He wanted an excuse to visit her every day. "But," he said, "she'll be vital when it comes to Peter Remington."

Liz took both her guns apart. She wiped each piece and placed the pieces in the precise locations in her sponge-filled briefcase. She said, "I think it's some terrorist group or some group with a beef against City Hall. I've made a list."

She lined up the empty casings in the box.

"Good. Tell me about it on the way to Shawnigan."

Liz closed the case, snapped the latches and locked it.

"Okay, McCabe, let's go," she said.

On the way to Shawnigan, Liz said, "I still think it was the right decision for you to visit Anna without me. She seemed quite taken with you yesterday. You can use that to your advantage. Probably it's because you rescued her the way you did. So if there is any more she's supposed to remember about the bombing and Peter, it's going to be you she tells."

Stu took a deep breath. "Tell me about your list."

"Okay. I've got five names here."

As she rattled off names, Stu was amazed that

Liz could keep so much in her head. She rarely wrote things down, yet always remembered everything.

"You know you're going to have to get these down in notebook form for all of us." In the rearview mirror, Stu saw another silver sedan. Was that the same car that had passed him earlier? *Curious*.

"Most of the people on my list have been fired from City Hall during the last year. Or people with grudges. One was a guy with several outstanding parking tickets. He was very distressed and said that everything was unfair, and when he walked out of City Hall he said that 'everyone would pay.' "

"That doesn't sound good." Stu looked in the rearview mirror again. Yes, that car did look like the one he'd seen earlier.

"That's what I figure," Liz continued. "Alec is going over that list as we speak."

"Has anyone talked to Johnny yet?" he asked.

"He's still unconscious in Portland. But you know," she said, tapping her knee. "In my opinion, Stu—and this is only my opinion—I think the person responsible for the bombing could have been one of the women the mayor was carrying on with."

"Excuse me? What women?"

She heaved a bit of a sigh. "Stu, it's common knowledge."

"What common knowledge?" Stu was getting

annoyed. Johnny and his wife, Marg, were his friends.

"That the mayor had affairs."

"I don't believe it. Where are you getting your information from?"

"You're a little touchy."

"The Seeleys are friends of mine. I rent from them, actually. I live behind them."

"You do?"

"I rent the house down the driveway from their mansion."

Johnny was an entrepreneur and wealthy, as far as Stu could see. He was also a bit of an arrogant loudmouth, but he was okay. Marg, his wife, was on the shy side, but surely Johnny wasn't cheating on her.

Often they invited him for supper and sometimes these suppers were matchmaking undertakings with various young women. None of these "took," however, because he was still single. Sometimes Marg would walk down to his cottage with a plate of muffins or banana bread.

They really seemed to have a happy marriage. Stu never saw anything but affection between Johnny and Marg. The extrovert Johnny supported the introverted Marg. "I don't believe it," Stu said to Liz.

"I hear the gossip. Do you ever notice how nervous Marg always is? That's a sure sign that a husband's stepping out."

Stu shook his head. "That's just the way she is. And gossips shouldn't be listened to." Why did he feel he had to defend the Seeleys?

"Nay, my friend," she said, putting up her hand. "Gossip is precisely our job. We listen to gossip, we evaluate. We find out what is fact and what is not."

The silver car was pulling closer to them. "We've got company," Stu said. "With your photographic memory, see if you can get a license-plate number on this car behind us. I'm going to slow down and hope he passes."

They slowed and the silver car gained on them.

"No license plate in the front," she said.

"Maybe they'll pass us."

But the car didn't. Instead, it turned right onto a street just behind them.

Stu pulled ahead, made a quick U-turn and tore down the street that the silver car had turned onto.

But finding the car would now be like locating a needle in a pile of hay. It was a residential street and right at the outset there were four roads where the car could have gone. After driving down various streets and looking for that elusive silver car, they went back out onto the highway.

Maybe it was nothing. But why did Stu have the feeling that it was something?

The hospital lunch was chicken noodle soup. The nurse raised Anna's bed into a sitting position and moved her tray up close to her. Anna picked up her spoon with her left hand, dipped it into the chicken noodle soup, tried to bring it to her mouth and tipped the spoon over. Hot noodles, chicken, carrots and peas slopped down the front of her.

She burst into tears. How was she ever going to apply makeup to people's faces when she couldn't even feed herself? She pushed her tray away. She wasn't hungry anyway. Her appetite hadn't returned, and all the meds she was taking made her feel sick. As best she could, she wiped the chicken soup from her hospital gown. But the tears would not stop.

Please, God, she prayed. *I can be so strong for other people—for Rodney—but I can't be strong for myself.*

She hung her head and let the tears come.

"Anna! Honey! Are you okay?" It was her mother who rushed toward her, saw the soup, saw the hospital gown and her tears and figured out what had happened. Catherine went into the washroom, grabbed a wet towel and started wiping her gown. "I don't know how they expect you to eat anything when you have that IV contraption hooked in your wrist."

Her mother wiped her eyes with a tissue.

"It's a good thing I came today. I brought a couple of your nightgowns. I thought you'd appreciate wearing something other than these awful hospital ones. I also have your glasses and some magazines, your Bible and a couple of books that were on your nightstand."

"Mom, can you look for my wallet at the cabin I was renting? I thought I had it with me that day, but I must not have because the police didn't find it."

"I'll look," Catherine promised. "I also brought your makeup kit. I know how much you like your makeup."

"Makeup." Anna lifted her left hand. "I can't even eat soup. How am I going to put on any makeup?"

"Well, we'll work on that today. Together." Catherine stood quietly for a minute. Catherine used a fresh wet cloth to wipe Anna's face. "Lois and her friend Marg, Mayor Johnny's wife, are here today, too. They're waiting to see you."

"Why would Johnny's wife want to see me?"

"She told Lois she wants to talk with you."

"I guess Johnny and I have something in common. We both survived the bomb blast."

"Everyone in church has been asking about you, and the pastor may come and see you. Marlene and Roy from the Schooner Café, too. Everyone is concerned and everyone sends their best wishes. Here." Catherine pulled closed the curtain around the bed and held up Anna's nightgown from home. "How about we get your hair washed?"

"I would love a shower," Anna said wistfully.

"I know. I'm having a guy from church come to

the house today to install a detachable showerhead in the tub. He's also going to install a couple of grab bars. They'll be installed by the time you get to my house."

"Oh, Mom, you don't have to go to all that trouble. And what about all your renovations?"

"They're done. The windows are in and you should see the little reading nook I put in the parlor. I think you'll love it." Catherine held up the nightgown and eyed the cast on Anna's right arm and the IV in her left. Wisely, she went to find a nurse. Together, Catherine and the nurse were able to take off the chicken soup–soiled hospital gown and slip on the fresh gown from home. They decided that her right arm would stay put for now, and they laid the nightgown over her right arm. When she was looking fairly presentable, Lois and Marg Seeley came into her room. Lois carried several plants. "From neighbors," she said, setting them down. Lois kissed her, told her that she was looking better than yesterday and that there was more color in her cheeks, while Marg stood at the end of the bed and simply stared. "Hello," she finally said to Marg. "I don't think we've ever actually met."

"We haven't."

The woman walked up and stood beside Anna. She knew that Johnny was in his mid-forties and she guessed that Marg was close to the same age. Yet the woman beside her looked older. Or maybe almost losing her husband had put that frown on her face. There were strands of springy gray in her brown hair, which looked to be cut in no particular style. The woman wore no makeup and her thin lips were pale. There were fine frown lines at the sides of her downturned mouth.

"How is your husband?" Anna asked.

Marg stood close to Anna. Her eyes looked fiery and Anna was momentarily taken aback. The woman seemed afraid, somehow. When Marg didn't say anything, Anna said, "I heard they took Johnny to Portland."

"That's right." Her voice was deep, guttural, a smoker's voice. "They'll be transferring him by ambulance to this hospital as soon as they can move him. Stu was here to see you earlier." Marg moved into the subject without missing a beat.

"Yes?" Anna was surprised that Marg knew about his visit. She called him Stu. She knew him, apparently.

"I need to know what Stu told you. I need to know everything you talked about." Marg sat down in the chair beside Anna's bed, while Catherine and Lois stood behind her.

"Hasn't he talked to you about what happened?" Anna asked.

"He doesn't want to. I know he feels protective of me."

Anna looked at her.

"Oh, my dear," Lois said. "Are you sure you

want to know everything? Deputy McCabe doesn't want you to fret or worry."

Marg looked up at Lois. "I need to know everything that Anna knows. You need to know that, Lois. Stu is my friend. He's our tenant, did you know that?" She looked at Anna when she said that.

"No. I didn't know that. He lives with you?" Anna asked.

"In a house that we own. On our property."

Lois added, "And poor Marg—she's taken on another boarder right now, which is just the worst timing for her, with Johnny in the hospital and everything." She turned to Marg and said, "I really think you've taken on too much this time, dear. . . ."

Marg ignored Lois and continued, "I came today because I need to know everything that Stu's told you. Everything."

Anna said, "I don't know how much I can tell you. Stu didn't tell me much. Just asked a lot of questions."

Marg moved even closer to Anna and whispered, "What did he ask you? What did he start with?"

This whole exchange was confusing to Anna. Marg seemed so demanding. But maybe this was simply out of concern for her husband. As best she could, Anna tried to remember as much as she could from their conversation. Marg didn't seem satisfied, however. She wanted to hear everything word for word—what Stu said, what Anna had said.

"I'm sorry, Marg," Anna finally said, feeling tired. "I think I've told you everything I know."

Marg shook her head. "I don't think you've quite told me everything," Marg said, backing away, "but that's okay. I know you have things on your mind. You and my Johnny are both survivors in this."

Anna nodded, dumbfounded at Marg's words.

After Lois and Marg left, Catherine said, "Well, that was a whirlwind few minutes. I wonder what she was going on about. Now you just stay there. I'm going to wash your hair."

Her mother headed out to the hallway and came back shortly with a nurse and a large metal washbasin and a bottle of baby shampoo. The nurse closed the curtains around Anna's bed, then laid her bed flat and helped Anna scoot up so that her head was leaning over the end. With a cup, her mother poured the warm water over Anna's head. It felt so good.

"My goodness," Catherine said after the nurse left. "There are still grass bits in your hair. And dirt."

"I must look terrible."

"You never look terrible," her mother said.

While her mother massaged the baby shampoo into her scalp, she said, "I'm worried about my sister."

"Aunt Lois?" Anna asked.

"She's gotten so close to Marg and that worries me."

"What's wrong with Marg?"

"I'm not really sure, but I think it has something to do with her church."

"What about her church?"

"She's quit the Whisper Lake Crossing Church, the one that you and I go to, and a few months ago started going to church with Marg. Since that time things have been different."

"What do you mean different?"

Her mother's hands became still on her wet head.

"My sister. She's always picked up strays." There was another long pause. "But it's not always in a good way. It almost becomes her Christian duty. But sometimes I fear she doesn't look at people as people but as projects, things to accomplish. I think she's looking at Marg that way now."

"What kind of a project is Marg?"

"I don't know her well. Lois hasn't told me much. I haven't asked. But Marg seems angry. And this was way before her husband was injured."

Her mother was drying her hair with a white towel. It felt so good to be clean.

"If you ask me," Catherine said, "there's entirely too much talk about evil in that church of theirs. They're on this big campaign about evil. I don't really understand it at all."

"Does Johnny go to that church, too?"

"I don't think so. I don't think he goes anywhere."

"That's too bad."

Catherine said, "I asked Lois once if I could go to church with her. I just wanted to see what was going on there. And she said no. It was a closed church."

"Really? A closed church? What kind of a church is that? I've never heard of such a thing."

"I hadn't, either."

Her mother stayed a little longer. They talked fashion while Anna flipped through magazines.

After her mother left, Anna tried not to think about her situation. Yet she couldn't help worrying about it. How could she expect her mother to wash her hair all the time? Would she ever get the use of her hand back? *Had God forgotten her?*

Midway through the afternoon, she heard Marg in the hallway. She lifted her head from the pillow. She recognized the woman's raspy voice. She was talking to a man, someone Anna didn't recognize.

She heard Marg ask, "And what's going to happen? What are your big plans now?"

And then the male voice answered in response, "It's being taken care of as we speak. There is nothing to worry about."

Anna laid her head back down on her pillow. *It's being taken care of?* What was being taken care of? Did this have something to do with what happened at City Hall?

FIVE

Lorraine Jonas, Hilary's mother, lived at 51 Rimshot Road. It was a small, detached bungalow, white with faded salmon-pink shutters. A porch, which looked like an add-on, took up the entire front of the house. A couple of Cape Cod chairs faced front and looked badly in need of paint and repair.

A diminutive woman with shaggy gray-brown hair and massive thick glasses answered the door. When Stu and Liz identified themselves, the woman sighed deeply.

She opened the door without a word, and they followed her into her front room. Despite the fact that the outside world was awash in autumn sun, the blinds were drawn and the air inside the house was thick and stale. A ratty green recliner faced a small flat-screen TV and beside the chair was a rickety metal TV tray with half a cup of coffee, a plate of toast crumbs and another pair of glasses. The television was tuned to a midday talk show. The occasional laughter seemed out of place.

"I don't know why the police keep coming," she said. "I've already talked with everyone. They already looked at her room and took her computer. I don't know what more there is."

Lorraine remained standing. So did Stu and Liz.

Liz said, "We are as concerned as you are about finding out who did this."

"I don't know who would want to hurt her."

"That's why we're here," Stu said.

Stu removed the blog sheets from a folder and handed them to Lorraine.

She glanced at them. "What are these?"

"Hilary wrote an online blog. In it she wrote about being threatened and stalked."

Lorraine handed the sheets back to Stu. "I don't know nothing about that. I don't know nothing about computers. The other policemen who came took her computer. Took all her stuff. Good stuff, too. Said I would get it back. Haven't heard a thing." Her hands were shaky.

Liz continued, "Did Hilary give any indication that she was being threatened? Do you know if she was afraid of someone?" Liz handed her another sheet, which Lorraine promptly turned over. It was plain to see that she didn't want to read it.

She said, "I don't know. She never told me."

Stu said, "So you have no idea who she was writing about?"

"I know she talked about her beauty school teacher."

Stu looked down at her sharply. "Her beauty school teacher?"

Lorraine nodded. "She wasn't too happy there. That could've been who she was writing about."

Liz gave Stu a look. "What makes you say that?" Stu asked.

Lorraine ran a gnarled hand through her bushy hair. "She never liked that lady much. Said she worked them too hard, was unfair and played favorites."

"How was Hilary doing in class?" Liz said.

"Not so good. She didn't tell me much, wouldn't tell me much, but what she did say was that she had doubts about their latest little project—the mock disaster. And see? She was right, wasn't she? She was afraid. It killed her in the end."

"Why was she afraid?" Liz asked.

"She just was." Lorraine paused a bit before she said, "I know that Hilary had no use for the mayor. That's for sure."

Stu asked, "Why not?"

"He made a pass at her. She rejected him and he has belittled her ever since. But that seems to be a habit with the mayor of Whisper Lake Crossing. I told the Shawnigan police all this, but they didn't put much stock into it."

"But why was she afraid of him?" Stu asked.

"I don't know why you're asking me this. I told the other cops all this. They even tape-recorded it."

Stu said, "We need to hear it again."

Lorraine went through what sounded like a well-rehearsed speech. She said that two years ago, Hilary had moved back home to Shawnigan. She ran her own beauty shop in Camden, Maine. She hadn't wanted to come back here. And since starting at the community college, she hadn't been happy.

There was a marked lack of emotion in this woman's words. She had lost her only daughter, yet no one would ever know it.

"Why did she come back here, then?"

Lorraine nodded absently. "I needed her. I had a room. She needed a place to stay. And I'm not getting any younger. What am I going to do without her?"

Stu wondered if his initial assessment of her was too harsh. People grieved in different ways. Maybe she was really mourning her daughter.

"Look at this place," she said. "Who's going to vacuum? Me with my back? I can't begin to do it."

"May we see her room?" Liz asked.

"Through there." The woman pointed.

"She's some piece of work," Liz whispered to Stu when they were in Hilary's room. Her room was like walking into a completely different world. The room was bright, smelled fresh and was clean. The bed was crisply made up, and the bottles of makeup and brushes on the dresser were neatly arranged. Travel posters, mostly of Australia and New Zealand, were on the walls. A beautiful poster of the Great Barrier Reef was bathed in light from the window.

While Lorraine stood in the doorway, hands on

her hips, Stu and Liz methodically went through Hilary's drawers, her desk.

"I don't know what you're looking for," Lorraine said from the doorway.

They didn't, either. But neither Liz nor Stu interrupted her diatribe. It would be handy if suddenly they were to find a diary written in Hilary's handwriting hidden in her sock drawer.

But they didn't.

"You see those pictures on the wall?" Lorraine added. "That's where Hilary wanted to go as soon as she got more qualifications."

On the way out Stu placed his business card on the table near the door and told Lorraine to call him if she thought of anything else. As they closed the door behind them, there was more laughter from the television.

Next on their list was thc apartment that Claire Sweeney shared with her sister, Lily. The tiny apartment on the south side of Shawnigan was bursting with family. Claire's parents were there, along with Lily, plus another sister with her husband and children. When she was shown Hilary's blog sheets, Lily said, "I didn't really know Hilary. I only met her a few times. Claire always felt sorry for her."

"Why?"

"Hilary had a mother she had to take care of. This is just a wild guess, but could this be about her mother?"

Stu had to admit that on the way over he did think of that.

"Or," Lily said, "what about her ex-husband?"

"Ex-husband?" Stu asked.

"Hilary's."

"Hilary had an ex-husband?" Liz asked.

"She was married. I think it lasted only a year. Claire said that once, I think." At the mention of her sister's name, Lily's eyes filled with tears.

Liz said, "But the blog uses the feminine pronoun."

"I'm just saying. I do remember Claire saying that one of her friends, Hilary, was sort of afraid of her ex-husband. And that's one of the reasons why she came home."

Liz and Stu looked at each other. Why had Lorraine omitted this important fact?

They got back in the cruiser and since Stu was driving, Liz called Lorraine and asked her about Hilary's ex.

They rode through the streets of Shawnigan while Liz talked.

When Liz finally hung up, she shook her head and frowned. "Some people," she said. "Lorraine said she didn't think it was worth bringing up. That it wasn't a happy marriage. Why mention it if it wasn't a happy marriage? So I asked her for the name of this ex-husband and she took her time but finally found the last address she had for him." Liz waved a little piece of paper in the air. "I got it. North Carolina is where Jack Habrowser lives."

"We got company." It was that same silver sedan in the rearview mirror. "I'm going to slow down again. This time we'll get him."

"Okay, McCabe. Do your worst."

He took his foot off the gas and the car slowed. The silver sedan sped up and passed them easily. A woman with a blond ponytail and wraparound sunglasses was driving. Two young children were in the back in car seats. On the back window was a little family decal, stick figures of a father, a mother, two children and a dog.

"I guess it was the wrong car," Stu said.

"Ya think?"

On the way into Whisper Lake Crossing, Stu turned down Front Street. "I'm going to the hospital," he said.

"Good idea," Liz said. "Maybe Anna will have something to say about Lorraine's comments."

He parked the car in front of the hospital in a stall marked "Official Use Only." The two of them walked in. Just as they were going to head up the stairs to the rooms, Liz said, "I think I'll wait in the coffee shop. You seem to have a rapport with Anna. I'm not sure my presence will add anything."

He smiled at her. "You're just looking for an excuse to have another cup of coffee."

"And you're just looking for an excuse to visit the pretty Anna. Actually I've got my trusty smartphone with me so I can begin looking for Jack Habrowser."

There was a bit of a spring to his step as Stu strode off the elevator and made his way to Anna's hospital room. He wished he'd brought her something—flowers, a teddy bear, something.

Anna was sitting up in bed and looked amazingly pretty. Her hair was soft and fluffy and her eyes behind round, red plastic glasses looked bright. She put down the book she was reading and greeted him with a big smile. "I can even see you now," she said. "I have my glasses."

"They look cute."

"You're being kind. They look weird." He had never heard her giggle before.

On anyone else her glasses would look silly, but on Anna they looked like they belonged. "Your hair looks nice," he said.

"My mother helped me wash it. But it's so flat now. I'm not used to it being like this." She fingered it with her left hand.

"You're smiling at least," he said.

"I laugh, and then I remember everything and I start to cry. I ordered new contacts today, but when they come in I'm not even sure I'll be able to use them. I feel so helpless. You need two hands to put in contacts."

"It won't last. You'll get better, Anna. Your arm will get better."

There was a pause in the conversation as they

both looked at the contraption that held her right arm away from her body. "So are you just here for a friendly visit or do you have more questions for me?"

"A bit of both, I guess. I talked with Hilary's mother today."

Anna's eyes watered. "How is she? It must be so hard to lose a daughter."

"Hilary's mother, Lorraine, said that Hilary wasn't happy with the esthetics course and didn't want to be a part of the mock disaster. Did she ever tell you that?"

"I gave her a choice. I gave all the students a choice. I did have a number of students opt out. They all worked on different projects at the college. No one who didn't want to be involved in the mock disaster had to be. I told them this was good experience. What we were going to do was make wounds look real. We had stage blood and all sorts of makeup for this purpose. They were getting special credit for this, plus, this experience would look good in their portfolios. But I didn't pressure them at all. As I recall, Hilary was one of the first to volunteer."

Stu frowned. This certainly didn't fit with what Hilary's mother had said. "Did you know that Hilary was married before?"

Anna looked at him thoughtfully and shook her head. "No, I didn't know that." She yawned daintily and put her left hand in front of her mouth. "Sorry," she said. "I'm on a new pain med that seems to be making me even more sleepy than the last one."

"Are you still in a lot of pain?"

"I don't think so. They keep plying me with pain meds, so I can't really tell. This time it's either yawn continually or be smothered."

"Smothered?"

She laid her head back on the pillow. "The first night I was here the medication I took actually made me hallucinate. It was the weirdest thing. I swear I saw a surgeon all done up in green from his head to his feet come at me with a pillow and put it on my face to smother me. I couldn't breathe. It felt so real."

"You had a dream like that?"

"I felt a pillow on my head. Fortunately, I had the wherewithal to press the nurse call button. And as soon as I did the nurse came into my room and the apparition, or whatever it was, disappeared."

"Just like that, it disappeared?"

"Well, when I opened my eyes it was gone."

"Who was the nurse?" he said, trying to sound as casual as he could.

"Sara. I don't know her last name."

They chatted for a few more minutes. Before he left, he touched her left hand softly and said goodbye.

He stopped at the nurses' station on the way out

and learned that Sara was working nights this week. He asked if the kind of pain medication that Anna was on could cause such real and vivid dreams, and was told that yes, it could. It happened frequently, as a matter of fact.

Stu was still unsure, but then what did he know about strong pain medications?

As he was waiting for the elevator, a person in hospital scrubs and a surgical mask made his way toward him, pushing a cart. The man was staring at Stu. There was something about his eyes that caused Stu to start.

Then Stu looked down at the cart the man was pushing. The cart was full of pillows. Pillows!

He thought about Anna's dream and shuddered.

To get to his little house, Stu used the same driveway as Marg and Johnny. He just drove past their large white house, past their spacious backyard with all its decks and fountains, and on down to the small green clapboard guesthouse he rented from them. He often remarked that even though his house was smaller, he had the better view of the lake. He was right on the lake, as a matter of fact.

Marg Seeley said that because it faced the lake, the deck on the green cottage was the perfect place to sit and enjoy a cold drink in the summer. Stu seldom did that, however. His free time was spent mountain biking, riding on his quad, hiking or mountain climbing. He didn't like doing nothing. If he did nothing he would end up thinking about his wife, Alesha, and how she had died.

So he kept busy. If he was working on a case, he would work on that long into the night. When he didn't have a case, he would watch sports on television, anything to anesthetize his mind.

The long lines of the sun were slanting over Whisper Lake when Stu drove slowly down the driveway past the Seeley mansion. Marg's car was parked at an odd angle to the house, as if she had quickly driven in, stopped the car and jumped out. Stu wondered why she hadn't put it in their four-car garage.

It seemed that every light in the entire place was on. And, should her front door be wide open like that? Maybe he needed to check on her. One of the things he hadn't done yet, but wanted to, was to head down to Portland to visit Johnny. According to reports, Johnny was still in a medically induced coma. He had broken his thighbone, lost a lot of blood and been transfused. They were also worried about his heart. He had almost died, were it not for the quick intervention of the EMTs on hand at City Hall, preparing for the mock disaster. As soon as he was out of the coma and stabilized, they would be transferring him to Whisper Lake Crossing Hospital. No one was sure when that would be.

He parked the cruiser next to Marg's and got out. He thought again about the person he had seen next to the hospital elevator, and the way that man had looked at him.

Maybe this case was making him a bit crazy. First, there had been that silver car. And then the man in green scrubs with a cart full of pillows. He had gotten mere hours of sleep during the past couple of days. That was all this was. A good night's sleep and he would get his perspective back.

Run in, check on Marg, then get home, plop himself down in front of the television and snooze.

His legs felt leaden as he walked up the wide steps to the Seeleys' front entrance. He didn't see her through the open door. He pressed the bell. No answer.

"Marg?"

He heard music. It was some sort of church choir music, and as he entered the foyer it sounded like it was coming from the kitchen. He called her name again. Still no answer.

The choir was louder in here. When Johnny was away on business, Stu made a point of checking in on Marg every day to make sure she was okay. By her own admission, being alone frightened her. She had even told him that one of the reasons they were so eager to have him rent from them was because he was a law enforcement officer.

“I just feel safe knowing you’re down [illegible] had told him once.

The Seeley cat came and meowed [illegible] ankles, loudly. He bent down and pat[illegible] head. “Hey, Spike, anyone home here?”

He was standing in the foyer, but didn’t want to venture farther and end up frightening Marg.

He called loudly, “Marg! Hey! Your door was open! You home?”

Despite the fact that the lights everywhere else were on, the hallway was dark. He called again. Still no answer. Just more meows around his ankles. He ventured farther.

He saw movement in the kitchen, faint shadows. He stood in the doorway.

Marg was sitting at the table, bent over a laptop computer and furiously punching keys. The frown lines around her face were more pronounced and her short hair was slicked back in pins. The loud choir music was coming from a stereo on the kitchen counter. Even though he was calling her name, she couldn’t hear him. Or she was so absorbed in her work that nothing else mattered.

He walked over and flicked off the stereo.

“Stu!” She gasped when she saw him and crashed the lid down on the top of her laptop so hard he was sure she must have broken it.

“Sorry I scared you, Marg. Do you know your front door is open?” On the counter was a bag of cat food. He poured some into a bowl for Spike.

dded water to the other bowl. Both were pty.

"Open?" Her eyes went wide. "I thought I locked it. I was just . . . I locked it. I *know* I did." She was fumbling for words. "I was just doing some work on my church's Web site. I work on it you know. I'm sort of self-taught on the computer. There was no one else who could do it so I volunteered."

It seemed to Stu that she was coming up with explanations and excuses that didn't matter.

She kept casting glances at the top of her laptop while she talked, as if whatever was on there would jump out and show itself.

"Marg?" He sat down across from her. "Are you okay? Do you want me to check around your house?"

She nodded. "If you wouldn't mind. I can't believe my door was open."

She picked up her laptop, clutched it to her chest and followed him around while he checked all the windows and doors. Marg talked as she walked.

"That girl," Marg was saying. "Claire. That one. She shouldn't have died."

"Two girls died, Marg."

"Oh. Two." Her eyes bright and wet. "They shouldn't have died, then. The two of them. So young. So much to live for. It's so very sad. And wrong." She shook her head. "The whole thing was a mistake. It should never have happened."

"No. It shouldn't have. How's Johnny doing?"

"Okay." She put one hand to her cheek, but kept the other firmly around her computer. "They say he'll be okay. In a couple of days they'll be bringing him to the hospital here."

"You've been down to see him?"

She shook her head. "Lois and I are going to go tomorrow. She's going to drive me. I just feel too shaky to drive myself."

"Good. I'm glad you have a friend to go with you. And, Marg, we're doing everything we can to find out who did this. And we will."

Instead of making her feel better, this assurance seemed to make her more trembly. Her eyes filled with tears. "Oh," she sobbed, "I just can't get my head around this."

Stu was reluctant to leave her. She seemed so distraught. "Is there someone I can call, Marg? Do you want me to call Lois to come and stay with you?"

She nodded, swallowed and then said, "Do you think Anna Barker had something to do with it? With killing those girls and injuring my husband?"

"Anna?" Stu was stunned. "What makes you say that?"

"She was there," Marg said. "She was the least injured of all of them. I've been doing a lot of thinking." She patted her computer. "Even looking up things on the Internet. She almost escaped. She would have, but then the building fell down on her. I don't think she counted on that. I keep wondering if she did this, if she is responsible."

Stu said, "Anna was almost killed herself. . . ."

"But that's it. That's it. The word is *almost*. She didn't die. I don't know, I just keep thinking about it. I keep going over it and over it."

How could she accuse Anna? That didn't make sense. And then he realized that he didn't really know anything about Anna. Could she have been responsible for the bombing? Maybe everything she had told him up to this point was a lie.

SIX

One week later, Anna was finally going to be released from the hospital. Catherine and Stu were at the hospital to pick her up. They would be driving her to the cottage her mother shared with her aunt Lois. Anna, equipped with physiotherapy exercises, was ready to begin again. The gashes on her face were healing nicely. Her white plaster cast had been exchanged for a fiberglass one with finger openings and a special pink cast over her hand.

She was told that her hand might require more surgery. It would probably be close to six months before she could use it well, and maybe a year before she got full mobility back.

She was glad that Stu had come with her mother to take her home. Lois hadn't come. She was with Marg and the two of them were home watching television. There was some sort of a television press conference that included the mayors of Whisper Lake Crossing, Shawnigan and DeLorme. The conference would be broadcast from Whisper Lake Crossing Hospital at Johnny Seeley's bed, after he had emerged from his coma. Two days ago they had moved him here from Portland.

As far as Anna knew, there were still no suspects in the bombing. But there might be suspects that

Stu hadn't told her about. She also knew they still hadn't found Peter.

She wasn't sure how she felt about that.

Even though she loved her mother, she wasn't looking forward to living with her and her aunt. On more than one occasion, Lois let it be known that she thought Anna's profession was frivolous, and not one that a Christian girl should aspire to.

Anna's temporary room would be the many-windowed parlor in the front of the cottage. With its large windows on three sides, it was her favorite room in the entire cottage. She and her mother had moved into this house when Anna was twelve. One of its features was a huge wraparound front porch. Catherine decided that part of the porch could be windowed in and turned into a solarium or parlor. Her mother had even added a little reading nook with its own overhead light. Anna was looking forward to seeing that.

"It'll be comfy, cozy and warm," she said.

There were two bathrooms in her mother's cottage. One was an ensuite off the master bedroom, her mother's room. Anna would be sharing the second bathroom with her aunt Lois.

Even though she would be recuperating at her mother's, she decided to leave most of her things at her rented place at Flower Cottage, which was only a five-minute walk along the beach.

She was hoping she wouldn't be too much of a bother to the two women, or they to her. She had come to relish her independence. During the past week in the hospital, the physiotherapist had taught her how to begin using her left hand more. She was practicing and getting pretty good at it. She could eat soup without slopping, and she had even learned how to care for her own hair. She hadn't mastered her contact lenses, but she was getting used to her glasses.

Over the last week, and to her delight, she and Stu had become friends. He was pushing her wheelchair now, her bags slung on his shoulder, and the intimacy of this act tugged at her heart.

He settled her into the passenger seat of his car, even though she said she was fine in the backseat and that Catherine should sit in the front. Catherine wouldn't hear of it, however.

Anna really did feel well. It was nice to be out of the hospital and in the bright sunshine of late autumn. There was friendly banter between the three of them on the way home, Anna exclaiming about the sun and her mother declaring how good it was to have Anna on the road back to full health.

When Stu turned the corner, she saw that two television vans were parked right in front of her mother's cottage.

"This is why I wanted to come with you," Stu said. "I had a feeling this would happen."

"What do we do? Why are they here?" Anna asked.

"My guess is they want to talk with you," Stu

said. He stopped the car. "I'll take care of it. You ladies just wait here for a minute."

A pretty woman got out of the van, along with a cameraman. Anna watched Stu walk over to her and pull out his wallet to show her his Sheriff's Department badge. Stu smiled at the woman. The woman smiled at him. Stu put his wallet away. It seemed to work. Because by the time Stu had walked back to the car, the van had driven away.

Catherine said, "My, you really charmed her."

"You're right, Catherine. I'm such a charmer," Stu said.

Anna smiled. She enjoyed the easy way her mother and Stu were getting along. Around the fourth day of Anna's hospital stay, her mother had suggested that Stu call her Catherine. Anna also reflected on the fact that during this past week she and her mother had gotten much closer, almost closer than they had ever been before. Stu insisted that Anna take his arm and the three of them walked up the front porch.

Leaning against the porch were the old panes of glass from the original windows.

Catherine looked at them and said, "Oh, good. I'm so glad the new windows are in. Everything is ready for you now."

"I can take this glass away for you if you'd like," Stu said.

Catherine waved her hand. "Oh, no. Don't

bother. I have a man from church coming to get it all."

"But this could be dangerous. There are a few sharp pieces here," he said, examining them.

"I'll call him when we get in. Maybe he can come today."

Lois and Marg were sitting in the living room with the television on when Anna, Stu and her mother went inside the cottage.

Catherine stopped when she saw them. "I thought the two of you were going to be at Marg's."

"Her television is broken," Lois said.

Anna thought this was strange. She was sure Johnny Seeley would have two or three flat-screen TVs in that big house. Here there was only one small television.

"Hello, Lois," Anna said. "And Marg."

"So nice to have you home, Anna," Lois said. "I like the pink cast."

Anna carefully raised her right arm. "It is kinda cute, isn't it? I had my choice of colors."

Last week Marg had demanded to be kept up-to-date on the case, yet today Marg's face was glued to the news channel. She barely acknowledged Anna or Stu.

Lois rose and said, "I'm sure you're wondering about bathroom arrangements."

Anna wasn't, but while Stu carried her bags into the parlor and Catherine brought her many vases of flowers into the house, Lois said, “Come with me and I’ll show you the bathroom situation.”

Anna followed her into the second bathroom. “You and I will be sharing a bathroom. We’ve got a new handheld shower attachment. We also had some grab bars installed, but you ask me, their placement is going to cause more trouble than they’re worth.” She continued, “This half of the vanity is mine. The other side and that towel rack is yours.”

Lois had moved all her bottles, hairpins, spray and pill bottles onto her side.

“It’s okay, Aunt Lois. I don’t want to cause any problems. I’ll keep my cosmetics in my bedroom. I’ll just keep my toothbrush in here.”

“Well, I don’t want to cause any trouble, either, but when you’re used to doing things a certain way for so long, it gets hard to change. I’ve already laid out your towels. Mine are yellow and yours are pink.”

“Oh, good. They’ll match my cast.”

When Anna had had the full tour, including what went under each cupboard and what went above, she followed her aunt back to the living room, where Marg was still staring at the television. “It’s going to begin soon,” she said.

Catherine and Stu were in the parlor and deep in conversation about the new windows and how “safe” they were when Anna came in. The parlor looked charming, the daybed was made up with a spread Anna remembered from childhood—one covered with pink ponies. For privacy, all the blinds were drawn. One of the far windows was open, letting in the warmth of the evening.

"It's almost press time!" Marg called. Anna went back into the parlor.

Stu followed Catherine into the kitchen to get some glasses of lemonade ready and Anna took the time to do a bit of one-handed unpacking in her bedroom. Anna had certain places she wanted to put things. Her Bible went on the nightstand, and the fashion magazines and novels she was reading would go on the table in the little reading nook next to the bay window. It would be a great place to cozy up and read for an evening on the easy chair.

She was about to join the women in the living room when she heard Lois say to Marg, "I just can't help but think that this whole thing is the beginning of God's judgment. It may be what we've all been praying for."

Anna paused, wondering what they were talking about. What was God's judgment? She was fairly certain the women didn't know she could hear them, standing as she was behind the door.

Her aunt continued, "We've been praying that God would send his fires of judgment on our immoral nation. The bombing of City Hall may only be the beginning."

Anna froze, felt her face go hot. Why was her

aunt saying this? Especially to Marg, who almost lost her husband in the bombing? How could her aunt be so callous?

Anna looked through the crack in the door. Instead of arguing, Marg was saying quietly, "But I didn't expect it to happen exactly this way."

Lois said, "None of us did, dear. But who knows the ways of God?"

Anna had heard enough. She couldn't let Marg suffer like this anymore. She entered the room. "Hello, ladies," Anna said as brightly as she could.

At that moment Stu and Catherine came in with a tray of lemonade and cookies. The press conference was about to begin. Anna wasn't sure she wanted to see it, but knew she would regret it if she didn't. She sat down on the couch. She took her arm out of the cotton sling and rested it on a pillow. Stu sat beside her.

Moments later the news program cut to Whisper Lake Crossing Hospital and the room where Johnny was in bed, his leg elevated in a full cast. He was flanked on either side by the two other mayors, and microphones were set up on a table in front of them. Each of the news affiliates made sure their corporate logo faced the cameras.

Johnny took the lead, as Anna knew he would. He always liked to be front and center of everything. "My friends, we have had a disaster, the likes of which we in our Whisper Lake communities have not experienced before. Our towns are peaceful. In our communities, you don't even need to lock your doors. That's the kind of place I grew up in. That's the kind of place I want to live in again, a place where neighbors take care of neighbors, the kind of neighbors where you can borrow a cup of flour in the middle of the night. . . ."

Anna tried not to roll her eyes.

"But, my friends and fellow Whisper Lakers, we have experienced tragedy." He paused dramatically.

"The tragic loss of two of our precious young women, the wanton destruction of our landmark building. My colleagues and I promise you one thing. We will not rest until these terrorists are brought to justice, until the safety of our communities is restored. . . ."

Anna leaned her head against the back of the couch, closed her eyes and didn't listen to the rest. She wondered if what Lois said could have any grains of truth in it. Could God be punishing her for something? Maybe going to California hadn't been His will. Or getting involved with Peter. *But I thought he was a Christian,* she argued with herself. *He told me that he and I shared the same values. Maybe I should've been more discerning. Maybe losing my right hand, even for a short time, is God's punishment.* She felt tears gather in her eyes.

"Are you okay?" Stu asked her softly.

"Just thinking."

"You know that can be dangerous."

"You're telling me."

When the press conference was over, Catherine suggested that Stu and Anna take their unfinished lemonades outside on the porch and watch the sunset on the lake.

Stu looked down at Anna. "If Anna's not too tired."

"I'm not." She wasn't, not if it meant spending more time with Stu.

Marg and Lois were still watching the news and Catherine decided to read a book in her room.

The outdoor two-person swing was something that her father made before he died. It had been sanded, repainted and repaired many times and was still in perfect working order.

"You grew up in this house?" Stu asked.

"I was born in Bangor. We bought this place when I was little. When I was ten, my father passed away. Eventually, we sold the house in the city and my mother and I moved here."

"Those look nice." He was pointing at a large set of bamboo wind chimes hanging from the roof of the porch.

"I don't know where my mother got those. They've been here forever."

He got up and gently rattled them with his hand. The sound the chimes made was deep and hollow and woody.

She took a sip of the lemonade. It was tart, just the way she liked it.

"How long has your aunt lived here?" Stu asked.

"Around two years."

She looked at her sandaled feet. He sat down beside her again and gently moved the swing back and forth. A long time ago she would sit on the swing, her father beside her, holding her hand. It was so long ago she was even forgetting what he looked like. But she would always remember his hand holding hers, always gentle, always warm. She told Stu about him.

He said he would have liked to meet him.

As they sat there chatting about inconsequential things, she was conscious of his presence next to her, the two of them brought together by tragedy.

"Are you any closer to finding out who was responsible for the bombing?" she asked.

"We're working on a few leads."

She looked at him and smiled. "Which means there are lots of things you can't tell me."

"I'm telling you everything I can. Believe me, Anna. I'm not hiding anything."

Anna said, "I know you're good friends with Marg and Johnny. How is Marg taking all this? She seems so confused. I really feel sorry for her. I was thinking of trying to get to know her."

"That would be good for her. She's taking this whole thing pretty hard. She's accusing me of keeping things from her. I'm not." He took another sip of his lemonade, and they talked some more.

Anna adjusted the blanket under her arm and noticed a movement in the parlor window behind where they were sitting on the swing. Maybe her mother was rearranging the room or unpacking. She should go in and tell her mother not to bother. She excused herself, saying she would be right back.

It wasn't her mother who was in the parlor room.

Marg's back was to the door and she was sitting beside the window, obviously listening to everything that she and Stu were talking about. Eavesdropping? Why?

"Marg?" Anna stood in the doorway.

The woman turned suddenly, saw it was Anna, opened her eyes and mouth wide, put her hand to her chest and said, "I just came here to sit beside the window and get a breath of air. I'm so used to just coming in here and sitting in this window seat. Oh, dear, I need to remember that you are living here now."

Anna wasn't buying it. The woman was clearly listening in on their conversation. Anna's emotions veered between angry frustration and sympathy. Marg shouldn't be in someone else's room, but she had a close friend who was calling the injuries her husband had sustained God's judgment. No wonder Marg was a little off center these days. She just wanted to hear what Stu told her about the case.

Maybe Anna just needed to give her the benefit of the doubt.

There were no new messages for Stu when he finally got home. Peter Remington hadn't called and the address for Jack Habrowser had been incorrect. All week they've been trying to find both of these men with no luck.

He had to admit that he was worried about Marg. Since the bombing, she'd been acting strangely. Anna had told him that Marg had been listening in on their conversation and also that Lois had told Marg that the bombing was God's judgment. He wondered about Marg's friendship with Lois. Perhaps that wasn't the wisest friendship in the world. But was there anything he could do about it? Probably not.

Now that Anna was home, he was worried about her, too. He wondered about her, too. So far, he didn't think she had anything to do with what went on, but Lorraine's words, and Marg's accusation, continued to haunt him. He thought of that entirely windowed room that Anna was sleeping in. Anyone wanting to get in the cottage would merely have to punch the glass in. Yet, short of putting bars on the windows, there was little they could do. Was Anna safe there? Had the bomb been meant for her? Had Peter Remington been involved? Where was that guy and why couldn't Stu and Liz find him?

Restlessly, he stood at his window and gazed out in the direction of Anna's mother's place and prayed for her safety, prayed for direction in the case.

Inside, even though it was late evening, he sent her a text message. Just checking to make sure you're okay.

A few minutes later his phone vibrated. She wrote—I'm fine. Thanks for asking.

He texted back—Be careful. Keep your doors locked.

She wrote—I don't think my mother ever locks her doors. This is Whisper Lake Crossing, you know.

He wrote—That's what I'm worried about.

Anna liked it that Stu was worried enough to text her at ten-fifteen just to make sure she was okay. She didn't have the heart to tell him that she'd been sleeping. Her cell phone vibrated and its vibration on the bedside table had awakened her.

This was her first night away from the hospital. No night nurse would be a call button away. So before she went to bed, she made sure her water glass was filled and that her two pain pills were right next to it, along with the bell that she was to ring if she needed her mother. So far she hadn't needed to take the pills.

She lay back down and soon fell asleep. A short while later she woke up, and thought she saw the shadow of a figure enter her room.

She closed her eyes and when she opened them again the figure was gone. It was just a dream, she told herself. Just like in the hospital, probably brought on by the medication she was taking. Except she was taking different pain pills now, ones that weren't nearly as strong. Still, she had been through a lot and the doctor told her it might be a while before she got over the trauma of the bombing. Bad dreams and nightmares could be a part of the aftermath.

She prayed and fell back to sleep.

When she woke up again, her arm ached. Perhaps she had slept on it wrong. She tried to ignore the pain. Tried to pray through it, but she couldn't. She would have to break down and take the medication.

She leaned up on her left side and flicked on her bedside lamp. Her water glass was empty. She stared at it. She was positive she had filled it before she went to bed. Did she drink it in the middle of the night? Or spill it? She leaned over and looked on the nightstand. No puddle of water. She looked down beside her. No water on the floor, either. The pills were missing, too. She suddenly realized that her bell was gone. How could that be?

She got up, pulled her robe around her as best

she could and got down on her hands and knees. The bell wasn't under the bed. Neither were the pills.

By now the pain in her arm was excruciating. She remembered what the nurse had told her. Don't try to skimp on pain pills. Don't be brave. Take them if you need them.

With her empty glass in hand, she groped her way into the bathroom. Because Lois's door was open, Anna didn't want to turn on the hall lights. But that wasn't a problem. Her mother had plugged a soft night-light into the bathroom counter outlet. Anna walked toward it.

A few feet from the bathroom door, she saw her bell sitting right on the counter and outlined by the eerie blue light of the night-light. How had the bell gotten in here?

She headed toward it.

Just as she was about to walk into the bathroom, she felt a sharp jabbing pain on her knee and heard the crash of glass. She called out before she fell forward toward the hard ceramic tiles of the floor. At the last minute she reached for the grab bar with her left hand and grasped it tightly.

Her mother was there in an instant.

"Anna!"

She looked up, dazed from where she was kneeling, surrounded by jagged shards of glass.

"What happened?" her mother asked, flicking on all the lights and helping her to her feet.

"I don't know," Anna said, attempting to pick the glass out of her legs. "I was just coming into the bathroom. Ow."

"Why didn't you ring the bell?" And then Catherine looked down. "Anna! You fell over this?" Catherine bent down and began picking up pieces of broken glass. "This is one of the outside windows! What's it doing in here? Who brought it in here?"

"I don't know, Mom," Anna said, attempting to rub her knees with her left hand.

"And why didn't you ring the bell?"

"The bell was in the bathroom," Anna protested.

"Why was the bell in the bathroom? Did you put it there?"

Anna said a barely audible "No."

"You just sit there." Her mother sat her down on the closed toilet seat. "I'm going to get a broom and a first aid kit. Don't move. We have to get to the bottom of this."

The commotion woke Lois, who stood in the doorway, her hand over her open mouth. "What happened here?"

"We don't know," Catherine said. "It looks like one of the old windows was leaning against the doorway into the bathroom. Lois, did you bring this window inside?"

Lois shook her head, eyes wide.

"Well, somebody did. And it wasn't me. This wasn't here when I went to bed. This is not good."

“I may have seen something,” Anna said quietly. She was sitting on the closed toilet seat and rubbing her knees.

“What!” Catherine stared at her.

“I thought it was a dream.”

“What did you dream?”

Anna told her mother and her aunt about seeing a figure in her room earlier, but that she had ignored it, thinking it was a dream brought on by a new medication.

“Well, this whole thing is a mystery, and look at your knee. It’s bleeding. You wait right there while I get some antiseptic and bandages.”

While her mother went into her own room to fetch these things, she and Lois didn’t talk much. Lois stood there, staring, her hand across her mouth, and Anna felt too weak and tired to speak.

When her mother returned, she went to work on Anna with tweezers, antiseptic and bandages. “Stu is on his way. He’ll be here in a minute,” her mother said, wetting a washcloth with warm water.

“You called Stu?” Anna didn’t know how she felt about that.

“He’s coming right away.”

Anna nodded. Was someone trying to hurt her? It was certainly beginning to look that way. Feeling a sudden chill, Anna pulled her robe around her more tightly. There had to be a simple explanation. She looked up at the doorway.

If the new grab bar hadn't been installed, she could have fallen on her broken arm and done even more serious damage. Just the thought of that made her cringe. She closed her eyes while her mother pressed the warm, wet washcloth to her knees and then gently began picking out the bits of glass.

"Lois, will you let in Deputy McCabe when he comes?" Catherine asked.

"Mom, I still can't believe you called him."

"He's worried about you and, frankly, so am I. When he left last night he gave me his card and specifically said that if anything strange or unfortunate happened to you, I was to call him day or night. How do your knees feel? I think I've got all of the pieces of glass out."

"They feel okay now."

A few moments later Stu and Lois walked into the bathroom, while her mother was coating her knees with antiseptic. He bent down and looked at her. "What happened?"

"I'm a klutz," she said, trying to make light of it.

Her mother told him.

Stu's eyes narrowed. "Where is the glass now?"

Lois said, "I swept it up and threw it all in the garbage."

Stu bent down and looked at the door. He looked up at the sisters. "And you have no idea how this old window got back inside here?"

They shook their heads. Stu examined their

front and back doors, plus all their windows. Stu kept asking questions. He quizzed her over and over about the figure she'd seen in her room. But she couldn't remember much. He asked her about the bell, and ended up putting it in an evidence bag and taking it with him.

Stu wouldn't leave until every window was shut and locked and the doors were double bolted. He also promised that a patrol car would be by periodically to check on the house.

All of this was supposed to make Anna feel better, but it ended up making her feel even more afraid.

SEVEN

When Stu arrived at the sheriff's office the following morning, Alec was on the phone. He was standing up, frowning. His voice was rising, and Stu hardly ever saw him angry.

Liz gave Stu an "I-don't-know-what's-going-on" shrug as he went to his desk. He decided that today he would find Peter Remington if it was the last thing he did.

The glass episode last night worried him. Was someone trying to harm Anna? He thought about her dream, the odd man she saw clutching the pillow and the IV, the pane of glass. All strange coincidences? He wasn't sure, but he would find out.

He opened up his notebook, but Alec's loud conversation caught his attention. "Why wasn't I contacted about this?" Alec demanded.

A pause. Then Alec said, "She's in my jurisdiction, however."

Another pause.

"You had no right to drive into Whisper Lake Crossing this morning and take her in for questioning, not without contacting us."

Stu looked up. Who was Alec talking to, and who was the "she" that he was referring to?

Alec said, "Deputy Stu McCabe was in charge of this case. He should have been contacted." A pause. "Oh, you can bet we'll be there."

Alec slammed down the phone. He looked directly at Stu. "The Shawnigan police came into Whisper Lake Crossing this morning and took Anna in for questioning."

"What!" Stu was shocked. "Why?" He had done nothing but question Anna all last week about the bombing. If the Shawnigan police wanted to question her further, why didn't they just talk to her at her home? Why come and drive her all the way to Shawnigan?

Alec said, "Seems they found something in her locker."

"What locker?" Stu stood up, almost knocking over his chair.

Alec was out the door. "Come with me."

In the car Alec said, "It seems that a firefighter found some fertilizer in her locker."

"Fertilizer?" Stu was trying to make sense of it. "What fertilizer?"

"It was determined to be the same kind that was used to make the bomb."

Stu's head was spinning. "I didn't even know she had a locker. Where was this locker?"

"She was assigned a locker in the fire hall in Shawnigan for the mock disaster. She didn't lock it, so a firefighter opened the wrong one by mistake. That's when he found it."

"Does she know where the fertilizer came from?"

"She says she's never seen it before," Alec said.

Stu clenched his fist. “Anybody could’ve put it in that locker. If it was unlocked, as you said.”

Alec nodded. “That’s what I’m thinking.”

“She never told me about any locker. Maybe she didn’t know she had one.”

“She knew, all right. One of her makeup aprons was hanging on a hook in the locker. In a pocket was her wallet,” Alec replied.

“She’s been looking for her wallet.” Stu paused. “Have we recovered all of her personal belongings from the crime scene?”

“We thought we did.”

Anna’s face lit up when Stu and Alec arrived. She was sitting at a desk with a police officer. Stu came over and crouched down beside her. “Hey,” he said quietly. “You okay?”

“They think . . . They found . . . I don’t know what’s going on. I never even used that locker.” Her voice was weepy and desperate. “The last time I had my wallet, it was in my bag. I know it was. I’ve been looking for it. I was going to go to the cabin at Flower Cottage and look some more. I don’t know how it got there. How did my wallet get into that locker? How did it, Stu?”

She looked near tears, shaky and pale. Alec was talking to the police officer, whose badge read Dennis Wilde. “Why did you think it was necessary to drive all the way into Whisper Lake Crossing and pick her up without calling us?” Alec demanded.

"The situation warranted it," Officer Wilde said. "This morning a firefighter found a small bag of fertilizer on the floor of her locker. Then he noticed the apron and the wallet. There were traces of fertilizer all over the wallet and the apron. Currently, we're having the locker examined for prints and we're having the fertilizer tested."

"That's not enough to bring her in and hold her," Alec said.

Dennis frowned. "We're not holding her. We're not arresting her. We're just detaining her. We just don't want her going anywhere. Right now she's a person of interest."

"Are you finished with her?" Alec said. "We'll drive Anna back to Whisper Lake Crossing."

"There's the little matter of Peter Remington. She claims that it could be this Peter who is framing her. But—" Officer Wilde paused and said quietly, "There is always the possibility that the two of them are working together."

Anna said, "I told them everything I know. I don't know where Peter is." She was clenching and unclenching the fingers of her left hand.

"We are actively looking for Peter Remington," Alec said. "Meanwhile, if you have no more questions, we'll take her home."

On the way to the car, she said to Stu, pleading in her eyes, "Do you believe me?"

He wanted to say yes, of course he did. And that was at the heart of the problem. He wanted to believe her. He wanted that more than ever—yet in that very deep part of himself, he just wasn't sure. Every day he talked with her, every day he spent with her, his feelings for her grew. He said instead, "Anna, let's just go home. We'll figure all this out."

Anna felt numb. She sat on the couch in her mother's cottage and looked straight ahead. Stu doubted her and that hurt worse than her arm, worse than the gashes on her face or the cuts from the glass in her knees. He hadn't answered her when she had asked if he believed her.

All the way home in the patrol car, no one had said a word to her. Anna had simply sat in the front seat and looked out the window. And then she had another thought. What if Stu had been pretending all along? She didn't have a stellar track record when it came to figuring out who was truthful and who was not when it came to men.

Maybe this whole week Stu had just been a police officer looking for information. That's all. Just trying to solve a case.

"You're not drinking any tea," her mother said to her.

"I can't."

"I'm sure that was all a misunderstanding. You'll see," said her mother.

Lois came into the living room, dressed for church. "I heard you had an ordeal."

"You might say that," Anna said, looking up.

"I'm on my way to Bible study. We'll keep you on the prayer line," she said and smiled solicitously at her. But Anna was really in no mood. "Why?" she asked. "When you think what has happened to me is all a part of God's will and God's judgment?"

"Oh, Anna, no," said her mother, shocked.

"Lois does, though."

Lois stood still, holding her Bible and handbag close to her chest, saying nothing.

"I heard you talking to Marg last night about all this being God's judgment."

"You were sneaking around and listening?" Lois accused her.

"I was in my room."

"What I said wasn't meant for your ears."

"What about Marg?" Anna asked. "Hcr husband almost died. Was that God's judgment? How do you think that makes her feel?"

"Lois!" Catherine said. "How could you, even for a moment, believe that?"

"You misheard," Lois said. "You had to be there for the whole conversation. I have to go. I'm late. It's not what you think." She backed out of the room.

When she had gone, Catherine said to Anna, "This is what I mean when I said I was worried about Lois—all this talk about God's judgment. That's why I'm so concerned." Catherine shook her head and went back to the kitchen.

And Anna was left alone with her thoughts.

If it was true that Stu had doubts about her, even a few lingering doubts, then she had no one to trust but herself and God. She was out of the hospital now and on her own. Maybe she needed to take control.

She took her cell phone out onto the porch and with trembling fingers she punched in the number that she knew so well. And just as she knew she would, she got Peter's answering machine. And just as she had done so many times in the past, she left a message. Only this time it wasn't those desperate messages of the past, *"Please call me. Where are you? I waited and waited . . ."*

This time her message was crisp and short. "Peter, I know you're there. It's imperative that you call me right away." She gave him her new cell-phone number.

Next she punched in another familiar phone number. When her California friend Cassie answered the phone on the second ring, her first words were almost a scream. "Anna! I've missed you. How are you? I've been e-mailing and e-mailing you."

Anna felt duly castigated. Cassie was one of her closest friends in California, her roommate, a woman who was probably the only one out there who really took the time to get to know her.

Anna said, "I know. I'm sorry. I've been kind of

out of it for a while. I had an accident. I broke my arm."

"Broke your arm! Oh, Anna. How?"

When Anna told her, Cassie's first reaction was, "That was *you?* That bombing's been all over the news. I can't believe you were there! I didn't even know where you lived. You left in such a hurry."

"I left you a note."

"Yeah, a little handwritten note," Cassie said.

"A long letter," Anna protested. She sat down on the porch swing. "Two pages."

"But you never said where you were going."

"I told you that I would get in touch with you as soon as I could. And that time is now. Cassie, do you have any idea where Peter is? Has anyone out there told you anything? The police are looking for him. They think he had something to do with the bombing. And I'm sort of wondering this myself." She got up from the porch swing and began walking from one end of the porch to the other as she talked.

"No," Cassie said, "and people around here are furious. He didn't show up to work. Tell me again why the police think it was Peter?"

"Because of his knowledge of special effects in movies."

"You're kidding me."

"Apparently not. He's not answering his cell."

"He never does."

"I know," Anna said.

Before they said goodbye, Anna made her friend promise to call her if Peter showed up. Cassie said, "No matter what anyone said, I thought you were one of the best makeup artists we had out here. I know it's crazy out here, but you are good. I wish you'd stuck it out."

When the call ended, she was standing next to the wind chimes. As she pocketed the cell phone, she leaned against them and they sounded. She looked up at them curiously. Why was she suddenly thinking about wind chimes?

Whenever Stu needed to work something through, he took his mountain bike on a long, hard, sweat-producing, muscle-burning ride. He had two favorite paths; one went up the side of Dragon Mountain along the road one way and the second went up the same mountain on the backside. Both were black diamonds, not for the faint of heart. He always came down the same path. He never varied his route. It was straight down the mountain, and he was always trying to beat his last time.

He had around an hour and a half until he had to be back at the station and he had things to think about, things to pray about.

He decided to cycle up the front side of the mountain. It was slightly steeper and rockier than the back path. Up near the top of the mountain, he could see the whole of Whisper Lake and then come right back through a shallow part of a rushing rock-strewn stream.

As he rode, he thought about Anna. She was a suspect now. Some very incriminating evidence had been found in her locker. And even though Anna seemed totally innocent, how well, really, did he know her?

In an investigation, it was wrong for a police officer to become personally and emotionally invested in a case. It was unprofessional and he should know better. And there was still the matter of Peter Remington. Where was he and was he somehow involved in the case? Were Peter and Anna working together? And what about Hilary's blog? How did that fit in? Or did it?

Halfway along the trail where he could see the lake, there was a straight stretch, a place where he usually coasted. He didn't today. He geared up and pumped hard, until he came to the next steep stretch. This was the part of the trail where most people bailed. But this provided him with the best thinking time. He shifted into a higher gear and kept pedaling.

Why did Marg think Anna was responsible for the bombing?

At the dip in the trail, Stu rode through the stream, splashing rocks and bouncing across the pebbles. He loved riding and the way it cleared his mind and let him think.

Soon, he was at the highest point of the trail. It

had taken him twenty minutes to get up here. He looked at his bike computer. A record. He had never made it this fast before. That should give him some satisfaction.

He stopped, breathed deeply and looked out over the panorama, down at the lake. A series of cumulus clouds over the lake looked like snow-capped mountains. If a person hadn't been told otherwise, he might believe that those clouds were actual mountains. He stared at them, breathing heavily for several minutes. Stu felt he could almost see Canada from here.

He'd been taught that what you think you see is not always the way things are. This was something Alec had tried to drill into him during the time he'd been at Whisper Lake Crossing. He looked at the clouds. Could he be missing some important piece of the puzzle? Could he be seeing things that weren't there?

God, he prayed, *help me to get it right. Help us all to figure it out. And help me to put my personal feelings aside.*

Ready, he took another gulp of water, set his computer and off he went. He felt good, he felt in control. His legs felt good. He didn't have all the answers, but he knew they would come.

He was racing down the hill now, trying to beat his old time. He knew he could. He had just rounded the last corner near the bottom when a slanted ray of sunlight reflected across a filament that spanned the path, as gossamer as a spider's web.

He had looked down just in time to see the wire strung carefully across the path and attached to trees on either side.

He braked hard and dirt flew up behind his tire. To keep from flying over his handlebars, he aimed the front tire abruptly to the right, and laid the bike down. His fall off his bike was controlled.

It could have been a whole lot worse. A thin wire had been strung carefully across his path, a foot off the ground, and attached to trees on either side.

EIGHT

Anna decided she needed to visit Marg. Her car was an automatic, no gears to change, plus, no one told her she couldn't drive. It might be a different story if she had to manually shift with her arm in a cast. Quickly, quietly, she pulled her mother's old woolen poncho over her head and made her way out the front door without her aunt or her mother being the wiser.

Now that Johnny had been transferred to Whisper Lake Crossing Hospital, Marg might be at the hospital with him, but Anna went to Marg's house anyway. It was worth a try.

At the Seeley mansion, Anna parked beside a silver car with an out-of-state license plate. She walked up the steps quickly and pressed the doorbell. It chimed richly from someplace deep within the house. Eventually a haggard-looking Marg answered the door. She wore a white terry-cloth robe that looked as if it might have belonged to her husband at one time. Every time she saw Marg, the woman looked older.

"Marg?" Anna said. "You said you wanted me to come and talk with you if I had any new information on the case. I have something."

"You do?" Marg was wearing a pair of skinny end-of-the-nose glasses. Probably she'd been reading when Anna rang the bell. She opened the door wide and Anna entered. "Someone is trying to frame me for the bombing. Someone put fertilizer in my locker."

"Tell me what happened."

Anna followed Marg into a richly furnished foyer and then into a kitchen beyond where a closed laptop lay on the table with half a cup of coffee next to it, plus some papers in a file.

"I was just working," Marg said. "Haven't even had a shower yet. That sometimes happens," she explained. "I get so engrossed in my work. . . ."

"What sort of work do you do?" said Anna, eyeing the computer. She'd always figured Marg lived handily off Johnny's many investments.

"I do Web design."

"Really?" Now that was surprising.

"Tell me about how you were framed." The intensity of Marg's voice caught Anna off guard. The woman seemed very upset.

Anna told Marg about the fertilizer, the locker, her wallet. Marg hung on every word. When she finished, Marg said, "So that's it?"

Anna nodded.

Marg took a sip from the coffee mug beside her at the computer. "Thank you," she said. "That helps. It helps for me to know."

There was a pause in the conversation. "What kind of Web sites do you do?"

"I'm working on one for my church now. I do the bulletins, too." Marg sat down and put her arms protectively over the cover of her laptop.

"That's very nice. I'm sure they appreciate it. How is Johnny doing, by the way?"

Marg shook her head, slumped in her chair.

Oh, dear. Had Johnny taken a turn for the worse?

"Oh, Marg." Anna put her hand on the woman's shoulder. "I'm so sorry. He's not well?"

"My husband is an adulterer."

Anna removed her hand. The vehement tone in the woman's voice stunned her.

"I can see that you're surprised. Don't be. I have to get back to work now."

"Marg?" Anna felt a sudden tenderness toward this woman. Although she had a beautiful house and beautiful things, she seemed so unhappy. Marg picked up the file folder and accidentally upended it. A bunch of black-and-white, amateurishly made brochures were scattered all over the floor.

Anna stooped to help her pick them up. "No, no," Marg said. "I can get them."

Anna picked one up. On the front was a picture of a square box building with the words *Dragon Mountain Church* printed on it. Marg and Lois's church? "Is this your church?" Anna asked, bending down to help Marg retrieve her papers.

Marg nodded, head down as she gathered the brochures quickly to her, as if she didn't want anyone to see. Anna wondered at this, but further questions about the church went unanswered.

Surreptitiously, Anna folded the brochure in her hand and deftly hid it under her poncho.

When she left, the silver car with the out-of-state plates was gone.

On the way home Anna was so lost in her thoughts that she didn't see the stop sign until it was almost too late. She slammed on the brakes and her right arm flew into the dashboard, stinging it momentarily. She pulled over and breathed deeply. If she was going to be a one-armed driver, then she was going to have to pay more attention.

During the sudden stop, she felt something fall forward from underneath her seat. She groped for it with her left hand. It was a plain black cell phonc. It wasn't hers. Was it one of her students'? Probably. Sometimes she drove her students home. She looked at it curiously for a moment. She looked around her. She was the only one on the road, so she stayed where she was, opened up the phone and turned it on, and then played with the buttons. There was no contact information, no previous calls recorded and no embedded text messages. She wondered about that for a moment before she put it in her glove compartment.

She had more important things to think about. She needed to get home and begin looking up Dragon Mountain Church on the Internet.

• • •

While Stu took various paths up the mountainside, he always came down the same way. And anyone who watched him or was familiar with his habits would know this. Carefully, he laid his mountain bike against a large tree and walked over to the wire. It was stainless steel, fairly heavy-gauge wire, and strung about two feet off the ground. It was attached to trees on either side with wire clamps.

If he hadn't seen it glinting in the sun, he would have ridden right into it. It could have killed him. And if it hadn't killed him, he would have been seriously harmed.

Not wanting to interfere with any fingerprints that might be on the scene, Stu examined the wire with a small stick he found on the ground. The wire clamps were expertly attached to the trees. This was not the work of kids playing a prank. Stu poked one of the trees with a stick. It looked as if it had been recently affixed. The bark under the clamp was green.

He opened his cell phone and called Alec.

"You won't be able to get up here with the car," he said. "Go to the Seeleys'. I keep my four-wheeled off-road quad in their garage. The keys are in the saddlebag. I think you should see this. I don't want to leave. And please bring the crime kit with you."

While he waited for Alec, he snapped pictures

with his cell phone. Near the tree where one of the wires was attached, he thought he saw a footprint. He took more pictures. He traipsed through the woods on either side of the path, careful not to disturb the scene. He was checking for anything that looked out of place. He found nothing.

He went back to his bike, sat on the ground and waited. He thought about how easily he could have cycled right into the wire. And that made him think of something else. The pane of glass that Anna had tripped over. Was there a connection between the two incidents? If so, why? Did someone want Anna dead? Did someone want him dead because he was getting too close to the truth about the bombing? Except he wasn't.

Could this be the work of Peter Remington? It disturbed Stu that they couldn't find him anywhere. The California police were looking for him. There had been no activity on his credit cards or ATM cards. It was as if the guy had vanished into thin air.

Presently, he heard the unmistakable sounds of his quad ascending the rough path. When Alec arrived, he took more pictures and looked through the woods.

"We'll look for prints," Alec said. "Or some identifying information. I'm thinking of bringing Steve in on this."

Steve Baylor was a former police officer who

sometimes helped Alec on his cases. He now managed a resort with his wife and two teenage daughters.

Carefully, Alec undid the wire from the trees, coiled it up and put it in an evidence bag. “I don’t know what this will tell us, but in light of what’s been happening, this had to be deliberate.”

Stu agreed. Alec bent down and looked at the footprint that Stu had photographed.

Alec said, “I talked with Jack Habrowser’s brother.”

“Do you know where Hilary’s former husband is?” Stu said.

“His brother says Jack is out with a bunch of guys delivering some sailboat up the coast. He hasn’t been answering his cell phone because he’s been out of range. Jack’s brother said that Jack was real broken up when he heard about Hilary’s death.”

“But not shook up enough to abort his sailing trip.”

“Apparently not.”

Alec shook his head. “We’re going to have to get back. We’re losing our light.”

Stu took one last look at the trees and wondered who had tried to kill him.

The buzzing of Anna’s cell phone early the following morning woke her. It was Bette, the Englishwoman whose cottage she was renting and who was graciously allowing her to keep her things there.

"I thought you should know something," Bette said. There was a worried note in her voice. "The police are here."

"What for?" Why would the police be at Bette's home? And why was Bette calling her to tell her?

Bette said, "It seems they have some kind of a search warrant for the cottage you rented. I don't know if they told you or not or if I'm telling tales out of school."

"The police are searching my cottage? Right now? Why?" Anna asked.

She sat up. This had to have something to do with the stuff they found in her so-called locker. Maybe they thought they could find more incriminating evidence among her personal possessions. This was all too much.

"Deputy Stu McCabe wouldn't tell me. I don't think he's allowed to. It's very infuriating, but I did overhear one of the police officers say that they were going to be going to your mother's place next. I just thought you should know. And if I get in trouble for phoning you and telling tales out of school, well, so be it. You've been through enough."

Anna looked at the clock. Nine a.m. She had slept in. She didn't hear anything in the house. Perhaps her mother and her aunt had already left. She needed to get up and get dressed. She needed to get over there. "Is Stu still there? I mean, Officer McCabe?"

"The last I looked he was down at your cottage."

"I'll be there in a minute," Anna said.

She dressed quickly and then headed out, walking along the lakeshore. Around the bend, she saw the police cars, two of them parked outside the cottage, which she had lived in up until eight days ago, hoping for a little bit of peace in her life.

Stu was there standing beside a police car, leaning into it and talking on his cell phone. He didn't see her at first, but when he did, he looked away.

Bette was on her porch, hands on her hips. When she saw Anna, she waved for her to come over. Anna headed up from the beach and walked to Bette's. "Bette, I don't know what's going on."

"I don't know, either. But come in, dear, and we'll figure it out."

Bette gave her a warm hug and said, "Whatever they think they're looking for, they won't find anything. You've been through so much. You don't need this."

Bette's kitchen was warm and bright and smelled of fresh bread. Through the window Anna watched as another van pulled into the yard. This one belonged to a television crew. Her friend Cassie was right. This was all over the news.

"Do you want to go and talk with Stu?" Bette asked. "I know the two of you are friends."

"We *were* friends. Something happened. He doesn't believe me anymore. He thinks my former boyfriend and I are in cahoots on this whole thing. That we planted the bomb, for whatever reason."

Bette stood and looked at her. "That's ridiculous."

"Tell them," Anna said, pointing toward the two police cars and one media van.

"I thought you and Stu had something special between you. Every time I visited you in the hospital, that young man was there," Bette protested.

"Things have changed." Stu hadn't spoken to her since she'd been detained in Shawnigan.

While Bette made tea, Anna sat down and told Bette about the episode with the windowpane, the bell being removed, about being driven to Shawnigan and questioned about some fertilizer in her locker. "I didn't even know fertilizer had anything to do with bombs."

Bette frowned.

"And then they think my former boyfriend, who does special effects for movies, is somehow involved. But that is just so ridiculous." She also told Bette about her strange visit with Marg.

"Poor Marg. She's had a difficult life."

"How well do you know her?"

"Not well. She's been in Whisper Lake Crossing ever since she and Johnny were married ten years ago. She comes from a rich family in Boston. I understand there was some trouble there, and that marrying Johnny was her way out of her family."

Bette seemed to sense Anna's turmoil and put her hand on Anna's arm. "I should phone my mother," Anna said. "I ran out here before I could call her and tell her what was going on. I don't know where she's gone. I don't know where my aunt Lois is. What are the police going to do when they get to my house? Are they going to go through all my drawers and things? What are they looking for? Why is this happening to me?"

Bette leaned over and put her arms around Anna and held her while she cried.

NINE

"It's obvious to me," Stu had said, leaning against the patrol car and talking on the phone to Alec, "that someone is trying to frame Anna Barker." The more he got to know Anna, the more he was beginning to believe her, that someone was behind this. Because surely Anna, in her condition, could not have climbed halfway up Dragon Mountain to string a piece of wire across the path—two feet off the ground.

Stu was trying without much success to keep his anger at bay. On the other end of the call, Alec was assuring him that they had to do this by the book, and that he, Stu, needed to keep a lid on things. What if, on the off chance that Anna *was* responsible, the police had focused their time and their resources on proving her innocence? Even though Alec didn't believe she was guilty, they had to face the facts. And, until the facts said otherwise, they had to follow the leads they had.

"What about innocent until proven guilty?"

"That's for the courts, Stu," Alec said. "We look at evidence. That's all we do. We collect evidence and give it to the courts."

Stu felt frustrated. He felt that Anna had nothing to do with this. "What about gut intuition?" Stu had asked. "You and I both know that she's innocent."

"Then the facts will reveal it," Alec said in an even voice.

The sight of Anna striding across the beach toward him earlier had flustered him. He didn't know what he would have said to her if she had confronted him, so he had turned away. He didn't know what else to do. He supposed that he would have had no choice but to tell her that, inside the cottage she had been renting, they had found a container of diesel fuel in a closet, behind a suitcase and under a blanket. It was determined that the bomb that destroyed City Hall was made of fertilizer and diesel fuel.

Stu had been in the station earlier when this particular tip about the diesel fuel had come in through the anonymous tip line. Liz had been manning the phone. She had spent a long time jotting down information on the pad of paper. When she hung up, she had said, "We've got some guy who says they saw someone who looked like Anna carrying a yellow can into the cottage that she rented at Flower Cottage. The person said he saw this person—who looks just like the pictures of the lady on the television—carry this in a month ago."

The Whisper Lake Crossing Sheriff's Department had no choice but to get a judge to issue a search warrant for Anna's cabin at Flower Cottage and for her mother's house, and for Anna's car. At eight this morning, the judge had signed the warrant, and they were here just before nine.

After going around and around some more and getting nowhere, Alec had said he wanted to bring Steve in on this. Steve and Bette and Bette's son, Ralph, who was a simple man in his forties, were very close. If anyone was going to get at the truth it would be Steve. Steve would be here shortly. And by now he was certain that the police were all over Anna's mother's house, as well.

Liz was outside now, standing in front of him, gesturing. "I have some more bad news."

"How could there be more bad news?"

"We found a cell phone in the glove compartment of Anna's car. We're quite certain it's the one that probably detonated the bomb," Liz said. "It's a plain black throwaway phone and we can't find out who it's registered to. There's no identifying information on it."

Stu stared at her. Whoever was responsible for framing her was really doing a bang-up job. "It's a plant."

"I agree with you. No one who does this kind of crime leaves evidence all over the place for people to conveniently find. It's just too coincidental. Plus, I don't know Anna as well as you do. I didn't go in to visit her every day she was in the hospital. But I trust you, Stu. I think the quicker we get to the bottom of this, the better. But, and here's the bad news . . ."

"I thought the phone was the bad news," Stu said.

"We have to go up to Bette's now and arrest Anna. Shawnigan's pushing for a quick arrest. And if we don't take her in, we're showing favoritism. It'll come out that it's because of you. Everyone knows you visited her every day in the hospital. The officer from Shawnigan took Alec and me aside and said that your behavior in Shawnigan was very unprofessional."

"Unprofessional! How was it unprofessional?" Stu exclaimed.

"They said when you and Alec went to the Shawnigan Police Department, you sat down beside Anna very close. Those were his words—*very close*. It was clear to all of them that you two were an item. The way you looked into each other's eyes, or something. So if we don't arrest her, it'll show favoritism. They want us to go up now and arrest her, based on the fertilizer in her locker, the wallet in her apron, the can of diesel fuel in this cabin and the cell phone in her car."

The two of them walked up toward Bette's house slowly. Liz said, "Just to make it easier, I'll do the talking."

Stu nodded. His mouth felt dry. He knew when he saw Anna's face that she would know he had betrayed her.

When Bette saw them at the door, she said, "You're here. Good. You can straighten this out.

Anna's in the kitchen. She's awfully upset. You can tell her that you found nothing of significance and she can go home and you can go home and everything will be all right."

Liz shook her head. As they followed Bette toward the kitchen, Stu's heart began that thudding again. It was almost as bad as the pounding in his head.

When they entered the kitchen, Anna looked up at him. She was still beautiful in his eyes, but he had never seen her looking so down, so sad and so thin. It seemed, despite her cast, that her shoulders folded in on themselves as she sat there, small, in her chair. Her lips were pinched and her face was white. She looked up at the two police officers expectantly.

"Stu? Liz? Is everything all right? Are they at my mother's house, too? I can't get hold of her. She's not answering the phone. They won't find anything. I didn't do anything."

I believe you, Stu thought but couldn't say it out loud.

Liz stepped forward and faced Anna. As Liz told her that she was under arrest and as she read her her rights, Stu felt as if he were falling into a deep, dark cave that he would never, ever get out of. He couldn't look at Anna, so instead he looked down.

Bette said, "Stu, this is ridiculous and you know it. Stop this immediately. Anna didn't do this, and you know it."

He only said, "We have no choice."

"You always have a choice." It was Anna who said this. Her voice shook with rage and fear.

In her wildest imagination, Anna never thought something like this would ever happen.

She was driven to the Whisper Lake Crossing Sheriff's Department in a squad car. She refused to look at Stu. Wouldn't talk to him. She sat in the backseat, looking down and shivering, while Stu drove and Liz sat beside him. Quietly, the two in front talked to each other. Anna didn't pay attention. When they got to the police station, they filled out forms and asked her more questions. She answered with as few words as she could manage. She was feeling sick to her stomach and weak, plus her arm was beginning to ache.

Liz took the fingers of Anna's left hand and pressed them into a pad of ink and then onto a card. The fingers of her right hand were still bandaged. Liz looked at them and frowned. It was clear that Liz didn't know what to do in this situation. Perhaps there was no protocol for broken fingers. They took a picture of her and asked her to please sit down across from Alec's desk.

The whole time Stu merely sat at his desk and wrote while Bette, who had followed them to the station, leaned over him, gesturing and arguing. Anna couldn't hear what she was saying. Her mother breezed in with a lady from church who was a lawyer. The lawyer came over and told Anna not to say anything. Anna shook her head. She hadn't really talked much at all because she was so numb from the arrest. She was not prepared for this surreal feeling.

The lawyer argued that because of her condition, Anna was not a flight risk. She said that Anna couldn't even drive. Anna, too downtrodden to correct this misconception, just kept her head hung low. Anna went over her story multiple times. No, the cell phone in her car wasn't hers. She had never seen it before and had assumed it belonged to one of her students. Her fingerprints were on it because she'd found it on the floor of her car.

After lots of discussion and telephone calls, Anna was finally released into her mother's custody at four o'clock that afternoon. When the television cameras tried to film her as she and her mother and Lois and Bette walked out of the police station, her mother put her hand up to cover their lenses and Anna dropped her head.

Anna had never felt so humiliated in all her life. Not even months ago when Peter had called her a "goody-goody Christian girl" in front of everyone they worked with at the studio. He was joking. He was always joking like that, calling her his "little hick from Maine," and then in the next breath he would bend down and kiss her cheek. Why did she take it for so long? The simple fact was that she thought she loved him. She thought she could change him. But not even when he declared to everyone that she wouldn't sleep with him had she felt this way. That had hurt. But this was utterly humiliating.

She felt debased and ruined. She could already see the headlines, her name and face splashed across the news. *Former Hollywood Makeup Artist Arrested for Double Murder.* They would show her before picture—her face made-up and perfect the way she liked it, her hair gelled and just right, the scarves she always wore at jaunty angles around her neck. And then they would compare it to the picture of her today. Broken arm, scarred face, weirdo red glasses, no makeup, flat hair and an old poncho of her mother's, the only thing she could put on quickly over her cast. No wonder Stu didn't find her appealing. It was stupid for her to think of Stu in any other light than a police officer looking to solve a crime. What did she expect? She thought she'd learned her lesson with Peter, but obviously she hadn't. Because here she was, falling hard.

Stu felt terrible about arresting Anna for murder. When Anna finally left late in the afternoon, she was surrounded and ushered out by Catherine, her aunt Lois, Bette and a lawyer. Aside from Bette, who spoke to him when Anna was first brought in, nobody else talked with him, not even Catherine, whom he had grown to admire over the past week. But how could he blame her? He had just arrested her daughter. When they had all left, he went in a back room to go over the case files again.

Now it was quiet in the station. Liz and Alec had already gone home. It was dark. Stu poured himself a cup of lukewarm coffee and went back to his desk with all the files and reports about the bombing. He reread all the police files. He read the news accounts. He went online and read everything he could. There was something the police were missing, some important piece of the puzzle that they were skimming over. It could be right in front of their eyes, but they weren't seeing it.

Could, perchance, Anna be guilty of any of this? Was he blind to the truth because he was attracted to her? She had told him that Peter Remington lied about being a Christian. Was that the truth or was that entire story a lie? Was Anna herself lying about being a Christian?

No! He pounded his fist on his desk. What about the pane of glass? What kind of a person trips over glass just to prove her innocence? Or maybe the glass incident was just a weirdly coincidental accident. And then there was Hilary's blog. He read over those entries again, trying to make sense of it. Were they somehow related to whoever was framing Anna? But why? He picked up the phone and tried calling Jack Habrowser. Miracle of miracles, the man himself answered on the third ring. Stu was so surprised he was flustered for a moment.

The connection was not a good one. Stu could barely hear Habrowser over the static. He introduced himself as the officer investigating Hilary Jonas's death.

"Such a sad thing," Jack said.

Stu told him about his ex-wife's blog entries. Did Jack have any idea who she was writing about?

"I thought you already made an arrest in that case."

How did Jack find this out so quickly? Stu asked him this.

"It's all over the news."

Oh, great!

Jack said, "I'm only guessing, but wouldn't she be writing about the woman you arrested? Look, I've been out of the loop for a while and out of Hil's life even longer than that. I'm only guessing."

"We'd like to talk with you. When can you get to Whisper Lake Crossing, Maine and go over a few things with us?"

"So the case isn't closed?"

"There are still a few outstanding issues."

"Well, I'm on the water. We're on a tight schedule. It'll be a while before I can get up there."

"Maybe we will come and get you, then."

"I've told you before. It's been a year since I even saw Hil. I don't know who she was talking about. I can't help you. I've moved on, man."

Stu wasn't backing down. "Still, we do want to talk with you."

"Okay, then." Jack's voice held something like annoyance, and when Stu hung up he thought to himself that he needed to check out Jack Habrowser some more.

Or maybe he was just grasping at straws, trying to find someone else to blame.

What more could he do here? He turned off the computer, put all the files away in their places, turned out the lights, locked the door and got in his car.

He thought about the cloud mirage, the mountains that looked like mountains but weren't. Maybe he needed to look elsewhere. What if someone were trying to kill the mayor? What if this person framed Anna for the bombing? Was Anna still safe? Was Johnny safe?

Stu didn't go home. Instead, he went to Whisper Lake Crossing Hospital. It was only seven. Visiting hours wouldn't be over for a while. Like Anna, Johnny had been questioned and requestioned since he regained consciousness. Like Anna, he hadn't seen anything or heard anything. But maybe Stu needed to try questioning Johnny again.

He pulled into visitor parking and got out. If Marg were there visiting her husband, then Stu could talk with the two of them.

He thought at first that the woman bending over Johnny's bed and kissing his cheek while he stroked her arm was Marg. But when she stood up and faced him, he saw that she was someone else. This woman was slender and blonde. Shimmery earrings dangled below her chin-length hair. She was wearing a pink business suit and heels. Stu thought he recognized her as the reporter who was outside the police station a few days ago. She held the back of her hand to her mouth, clearly embarrassed to be caught in such a compromising position.

Stu thought about what Liz had said, that Johnny was a philanderer. Stu had not believed Liz. But here was the evidence.

Johnny broke the silence. "This is Chloe. She works for the Augusta TV station."

Stu nodded. "Hello. I've seen you."

"She's very good," Johnny said. "She was just dropping off some papers for me to go over. From the TV station. She's arranging another press conference. Do you know she single-handedly got that press conference set up? She's a little go-getter."

"Johnny," Chloe said, "I've got to be going."

After Chloe left, Stu just stood there.

"It's not what you think," Johnny said.

"I'm not thinking anything. What you do with your life is your own business."

Johnny hooked his finger, motioning Stu to come closer. When Stu was within whispering distance, Johnny said, "Listen, Stu, it's time you knew something about Marg. Marg is a great woman. I love her to death. I really do, but I married her when I was a different person. I've moved on and she's stayed behind. And lately, all she thinks about is her stupid church. She won't do anything without her church's permission. The minister has Marg under his thumb, along with every other member. It's dangerous, and I've tried to reason with her, but it does no good. She's set in her ways, and I can't change them. I've already told her that if she does not want to be my wife I will look elsewhere."

Stu had always admired Johnny and Marg. He had spent so many evenings in their home. But then he tried to remember. When was the last time he had been invited to supper with Marg and Johnny? It had been a good nine months to a year. He knew Marg was going to church somewhere. It wasn't the church that he went to. There weren't that many churches in Whisper Lake Crossing. "What church is she going to?"

"Some church on Dragon Mountain Road. I've never been there. Have no desire to go."

Dragon Mountain Road. Up past Dragon Mountain Road was where he mountain-biked.

There was a cement building up there with a sign outside the front that referred to some sort of a church, but Stu had never paid much attention to it.

"When did Marg start going to this church?" Stu asked.

"It has to be almost a year ago now. And it's not a church, it's a cult. I've tried to use my influence in City Hall to get it shut down. But Dragon Mountain is just outside the city limits."

Stu was sure that Johnny was deftly changing the subject, deftly trying to move the blame for his behavior from him to some church, but he let Johnny talk. "I mean it, when somebody starts talking about crime and terror as if this is God's judgment or God's doing it, that's the day I walk out of church and don't go back."

Stu did want to remind Johnny that even though his wife was mixed up in a church group, that didn't give him the right to go out and have affairs, but he didn't. Stu asked, "How are you feeling, Johnny?"

"Getting better. A little bit at a time."

"I came to ask you about enemies. I came to ask who you think might have set that bomb. Liz gave you a list of people with beefs against City Hall. Have you had a chance to go over that list yet?"

"I thought you made an arrest in that case, so why do you need this list?"

"Just clearing up some loose ends," Stu replied.

Later, when Stu stood by the elevator, he remembered the man in green scrubs who had stared at him so intently on his first visit here. He shook off that memory and headed for home.

His thoughts roiling, he turned into the long driveway that led past the Seeley mansion and down to his cottage. A silver car was parked in the far corner of Marg's circular driveway. He stared at it. Then pulled in beside it and went to have a look at it. He jotted down the license number. It was from out of state.

The front door opened and Marg came out. "Nice car, Marg. I didn't know you got a new one."

Hands wringing, Marg told him the car belonged to her new boarder.

"You have a boarder?" he asked.

She nodded. "He's staying in the apartment in the basement."

It was funny that Johnny didn't mention this when he was there. "How long has your boarder been here?"

Marg shrugged and looked away when she said, "Oh, a few days now."

"Who is it?"

"Just someone from my church who needed a place to stay."

"What's his name? Can I meet him?"

Marg seemed cagey when she said, "You can knock on his door, but I don't think he'll answer.

When he gets busy with his study and work, he doesn't seem to answer."

Stu went to the basement door and knocked. Just as Marg had said, there was no answer. The basement apartment, which had never been rented out in the two years Stu had lived here, had a number of small windows at ground level. He walked past each one. They were all curtained shut.

Marg was standing by the front door and said, "I don't know him very well. He might be out for a walk. He often walks along the beach or hikes."

"He's not answering his door. How about if I sit on your porch and wait for him?"

"Sometimes he's gone for hours, Stu. I don't know where he goes. I could tell him you're looking for him." She kept her eyes averted as she spoke. Her eyes looked wet and she sniffed several times. Stu thought about the woman he'd seen in Johnny's hospital room and felt sorry for her. He wished he could help.

Did Marg have any idea who that woman was? Stu doubted it, but he also had a feeling that Marg suspected something, knew something. And he wondered what all of this had to do with the bombing.

TEN

Anna sat on the porch swing and tried not to think about the fact that the last time she was in this spot, Stu was with her. As he'd gently moved the swing back and forth with his foot, they'd drunk lemonade and talked and talked. It was warm that evening as they had watched the sun go down.

It was too cool and windy to be sitting outside now, but somehow the cold felt good. She watched one maple leaf skitter across the front lawn. Beyond it the flag on the pole down by the lake stood flat out in the wind. Next to her on the seat, the pages of her Bible fluttered in the breeze. She put her hand on the cover to still it. Earlier she had read a passage in Psalms that gave her some comfort. David was blamed for things he didn't do. He'd been angry about that, really seething at God, and yet he was called "a man after God's own heart."

God, I don't know why I'm in this position right now, she prayed. *But if there's something for me to learn, help me to get over my anger and frustration and learn it.*

She gazed out at the lake, waves skidding across its surface. The hollow wooden tubes of the wind chimes echoed loudly in the wind. Every time she looked at them, she had a strange inkling that there was something about the wind chimes that was important. She couldn't bring up to the surface of her consciousness what it was, though. The chimes were old, and had seen many Maine winters. She couldn't remember a time when they weren't hung from that hook on this corner of this porch.

She hugged her mother's woolen sweater around her and put the Bible on her lap to keep the pages from flapping. The night she had fallen in the bathroom, she had heard the faint sounds of the wind chimes. She had fallen back to sleep then. The next time she got up her bell was gone, her water glass was empty and she had crashed into glass on the bathroom floor.

That night when she and Stu drank lemonade on the porch was a still night. Stu had even commented on it. Yet, during that night she had heard the faint, hollow sound of the wind chimes. That meant that someone, or something, had caused the wind chimes to sound that night. And if it was a someone, it was someone who had come in from the outside, someone who knew her mother never locked the front door, someone who knew about her bell and her glass of water and her pills.

She knew someone was deliberately framing her. Someone had purposely walked up on the porch and bumped into the wind chimes before coming inside the house. Was it someone who didn't know the wind chimes were there? Possibly.

Peter? But why?

She needed to do some more research on her own. Since the police had taken her computer, she would go where there were computers.

She took her Bible inside, grabbed her keys from her nightstand and walked out to her car.

The Schooner Café had WiFi access, plus a couple of computers along the back wall for use by patrons. She ordered a large house-blend coffee and sat down at one of the computers.

Marlene, the owner of the café, came over, took the seat beside her, put her hand on Anna's left arm and said, "How are you doing, my dear?" There was real concern in her eyes.

Anna said, "Just dandy."

"Oh, dear."

"Actually," Anna said, "I'm not doing as bad as you might think. I'll be okay. I know I will. I had a good talk with God this morning. I'm just trying to figure a few things out."

"Well, that's good. I've been praying for you, honey. I should think the police would be working overtime to prove that you had nothing to do with the bombing. These charges are ridiculous. Everybody in Whisper Lake knows it. Everyone in the church does, too."

"Thank you." Anna knew she had the support of the people in town.

Marlene's eyes narrowed, as if she were thinking hard about something. "What's the matter?" Anna asked.

"You have one of those brochures," Marlene said. Next to the computer was the Dragon Mountain Church brochure. Anna intended to do more research into it, as well. Marlene picked it up. "I know this church. These brochures have been left around here on tables. Someone from this church even wanted to put up a poster here. I said no."

Anna said, "My aunt has been going there. So has Marg Seeley."

"I work here. I know all the gossip about that place." Marlene lowered her voice. "I can't help but think that Marg Seeley is on the verge of some sort of nervous breakdown or something."

"Really?"

"I have this feeling that Marg knows something about the bombing, and that it's scaring her to death. Maybe she is even protecting someone."

"Really? You should talk to Alec or Stu about that."

"What would I say? It's just an impression, woman's intuition. About a year or so ago, Marg came to me. She was thinking about leaving Johnny because he was cheating on her. I told her to go and talk to the pastor. I mean, I'm no marriage counselor. Shortly after that she hooks up with Dragon Mountain Church. And she and

Johnny stayed together, so I just assumed they'd worked things out." Marlene lowered her voice. "I know your aunt goes there, too. Maybe she could help Marg through whatever it is she's trying to work through."

Anna said, "And you think this has something to do with the bombing?"

"I feel that Marg either knows something, is protecting someone or is afraid for her life. And I sort of . . ." Marlene bit her lower lip. "I sort of have a feeling that you are in some kind of danger."

Anna shrugged and gave Marlene a bit of a smile. She had a broken arm, no job and she'd been arrested for murder. What else could possibly happen to her? She said, "You don't know the half of it. Right now, though, all I can do is do what I can do and leave the rest in God's hands."

"That's a good attitude," Marlene said, rising and patting Anna's shoulders. "How's the arm, anyway?"

Anna looked up at her. "Oh, you mean the least of my worries?" she said, lifting her right arm. "It's getting better, I think. I have an appointment in a few days to get it looked at. I'll know more then."

"I'll be praying for that, too." Marlene patted Anna on the shoulder and left.

Anna called it the least of her worries, yet even

now her arm ached. She could barely move her fingers at the end of her cast. She also tried not to think about the fact that there was such a long haul before she would be any better.

Stu was driving through Whisper Lake Crossing when he saw Anna's car parked at the Schooner Café. Good. He wanted to talk to her. He drove around the side and parked between two pickups. He chirped his car door lock in time to see Anna get in her own car and drive away.

He called after her, but of course she couldn't see him, much less hear him. It also appeared that Anna was deep in thought. She was probably on her way home. Stu would backtrack and follow her.

He watched her car take the exit out of town. Quickly he got into his car, and turned and followed her as she drove out of town.

There were a few cars separating his car from Anna's. Maybe that was good. If she knew he was following her, then she might speed up or flee. He kept driving, and followed Anna's car as she headed out onto the highway.

"Anna, Anna, where are you going?" he said out loud. A panel truck separated their cars now, which again was a good thing. It would be hard for Anna to see his car in her rearview mirror. Every once in a while, he caught a glimpse of her and that was enough.

It was windy on the highway and his little car rocked to and fro a few times. Along the side of the highway, scrub brush danced frantically in the wind. She was going to Shawnigan. There was no doubt about that now. Her right blinker was on. She took the first exit to Shawnigan.

He followed her down the same exit. He wondered if she was going to visit Rodney or one of her other students. Or maybe she had an appointment with someone at the college about returning to work. He half expected her to take the turn that led to the community college.

She didn't.

Instead, he found himself following her along the main street next to the railroad tracks, which led to City Hall. By now he was pretty sure she knew he was behind her. He had seen her glance up at her rearview mirror a few times. When she parked next to the blasted-out City Hall building, he pulled up right beside her. She looked over at him, frowned and turned back to her steering wheel without expression.

He watched her get out of her car and walk over to the building. Back still to him, she made her way to the part of the stone fountain that had not been razed by the bomb blast. She sat down on one edge of the fountain and looked fixedly into the broken building. She did not turn to see if he followed her.

He held back. For a while he stood beside his car

and looked at the building. Even though he had driven past this place many times the previous week, this time he allowed himself to really look at it, maybe through her eyes.

What did she see when she looked at the ruins of this building?

A place where she almost died?

Much of the building was boarded up and surrounded by yellow crime-scene tape, the edges of which blew noisily in the strong breeze. It looked like a giant cutaway, with rooms clearly visible. Much of the furniture was still there. Stu knew that Forensics was still going over it, bit by bit and piece by piece. He was surprised that no one was here now, warning Anna away and telling her she was too close, that she wasn't allowed to be here.

Stu went over and sat down beside her.

"What are you doing here?" she said without looking at him. "Don't you know I'm a criminal?"

"Anna . . ."

"I'm a felon. I should be in jail. Just ask anyone you work with."

"Why did you come here, of all places?" Stu looked at her profile. Her eyes under her glasses were filling with tears. Right now he wanted to take her in his arms and tell her that everything would be okay.

"I came here," she said, looking at the building, "because I was hoping it would help me remember something. I remembered about the wind chimes today and I thought maybe coming here would help me remember about what happened."

He looked at her curiously. "What wind chimes?"

"On the night that I fell onto the glass windowpane, I heard the wind chimes on my mother's porch. I heard them quite distinctly. But that was a still night. Not like now. So, I think that the windowpane was put there by someone who came onto the porch from the outside."

Stu listened. "I remember. It wasn't windy that night at all." He thought about that, wondered at the significance. He turned to her. She was looking at him square on. He asked her, "Was this what you came here to remember?"

She looked back at the building and shook her head. "I didn't do it, you know. I wish you would believe me. . . ."

Stu was about to say what he had come here to say when she went on. "There was someone running," she said. "My mind was so distracted that morning. Johnny was walking in with me and I didn't really like being with him very much. So I was concentrating on getting away from him because I had a lot on my mind. I wanted to talk to Hilary. She was having problems, and I was holding my coffee and had a million things to do."

Stu waited.

"I don't think this bombing has to do with me. I think I just got in the way of what was really happening. This has to do with Johnny Seeley and Hilary Jonas."

"In what way?" he asked. A patch of sunlight shimmered down on the two of them from a narrow break in the clouds. There were freckles on Anna's nose that he'd never noticed before. He found himself staring at them. Their faces were so close that for one moment he wanted to take that face between his hands and kiss her.

She took something out of her pocket, unfolded it and handed it to him. "I found this at Marg's house. She had a pile of them. She was working on her church's Web site."

He took the threefold brochure from her. It was for a new church in Whisper Lake Crossing. The address was Dragon Mountain, where he always biked.

Anna said, "I went on the church Web site, and a lot of it is very confusing. There is this constant talk about 'getting rid of evil, getting rid of evil.' It's like a broken record and I really didn't know what it meant. I didn't know how they were going to rid the world of evil. Well, I clicked through some links. It looks like what they advocate is 'praying hard for God's judgment to fall.'" She took back the brochure and pointed to a Web link on the back of the brochure. "And I found out that they look at natural disasters and man-made disasters as evidence of this judgment, and thus, getting rid of evil and evil people."

"That's kind of dangerous thinking," Stu said.

"This link talks about global disasters—fires and volcanoes—and about how specifically they are God's judgment. I was looking this up on the Web at the Schooner Café. Since I can't write anything, I tried to memorize as much as I could."

Stu nodded.

"Actually, I got into a Members Only section of the Web site that explained all this. It's not out there for the general public."

"How'd you get in?"

"I figured my aunt Lois was a member, so I used her e-mail address, and then I clicked on the 'Forgot Your Password?' link. It wasn't a very secure site, and within moments I was able to change both my aunt's e-mail and her password."

"Don't you think she'll notice?"

Anna shook her head. "She and my mother share a computer. She's not on it all that much. But the Web site lists specific disasters and names specific people that God supposedly wanted to 'judge.' It was horrific. And the Web site specifically mentioned Johnny Seeley as someone who God wanted to judge."

"Anna." Stu stared at her. "This is important."

"I know. It proves that some people weren't too

unhappy about his being caught up in the bombing, but it still doesn't prove who did it."

"Still . . ."

"Marg has been acting so frightened lately. I'm thinking she knows what her church has said about her husband."

"Why did you come out here instead of coming directly to me with this information?"

"I'm telling you now." She looked directly at him. "Hilary Jonas was also on that list."

"Did this Web site say why these people were on the list?" Stu asked.

She shook her head. "I can sort of understand why he was on that list. I know Johnny a little bit. I grew up in this town. Johnny was always into one questionable business deal after another. But he always comes out, as he does now, smelling like a rose."

She looked up at Stu. "I came out here because I thought it would help me remember. Maybe Johnny is behind whoever has been framing me. I think Marg might know something. I think she's afraid. I . . ." She paused. "I know what that's like. I didn't do this, Stu."

Stu looked at her intently and said, "I came here, I followed you because I wanted to tell you that I believe you. I know you're innocent. I do believe you. Arresting you was a mistake."

She stared at him for several more minutes before she whispered, "You believe me?"

“I do.” And in so saying, Stu knew he was putting himself in a compromising position. He was a police officer. It was his job to remain objective. And, of course, there was all that evidence against her. He didn’t know what he was going to do about that.

ELEVEN

On the way home, Anna plugged a CD into her car stereo and thought about Stu. Earlier, when they sat beside each other on the damaged cement fountain, he had been close enough to kiss her. For a moment, she thought he actually would. But he didn't.

She had to remind herself that he was just investigating a case. How could she be certain that he wasn't still playacting? But the way he had said *I believe you* sounded as if he really meant it.

Maybe he did.

Maybe he didn't.

Anna needed to guard her heart. She couldn't, she wouldn't be hurt again. She had believed enough lies to last a lifetime.

Time to turn your thoughts away from that man in the car ahead of you, she admonished herself. Instead, she thought about all she had learned at the Internet café today, all the disturbing things about the church that her aunt was involved in. What disturbed her the most, what she couldn't understand was that Johnny Seeley and Hilary Jonas were on the church's "list."

She had hoped that by sitting in front of the City Hall building something would jog her memory. It almost had. But then Stu had showed up. Every time she was near him it was like her brain short-circuited, and she couldn't think straight.

He was ahead of her on the highway. Think, she admonished herself. She had seen someone just before the building had fallen down around her. Her mind kept going back to Peter. But was it Peter?

At home, Catherine was putting on her coat.

"You're going out this evening?" Anna asked.

Catherine seemed flustered. She was rattling her car keys nervously. "Oh, dear. I know I should go. I know I should go and find out what's going on, but I'm not sure. Lois and Marg just left for a church meeting. I asked Lois if I could come and she said it would be better if I didn't. But I thought I would go anyway. What is she trying to hide? I'm getting really concerned about my sister. What do you think? Do you think I should go?"

"I'll come with you. Let's go."

After a few false starts and a drive up Dragon Mountain on the wrong road for half a mile, they finally found the building. Anna had decided not to call it a "church" anymore. She called it a building.

The building was small and square and constructed out of cement blocks.

"This old place," Catherine said. "This used to be an auto body shop. Can't believe someone would convert this into a church."

"It's not a church," Anna said.

Her mother looked at it. “But there is the sign,” Catherine pointed.

“No, Mother, what I’m saying is that I don’t think this qualifies as a church. I think I would call it a cult.”

“Oh, dear, and to think Lois . . .” She didn’t finish her sentence.

By the time she and her mother parked, the service was in session. Anna and Catherine were outside and could already hear the shouting.

“Oh, my,” Catherine said. “Our minister never speaks that loud.”

“That’s a good thing.”

Inside it was bright and hot. At the front, a short, sweaty man with his white shirtsleeves rolled up was pacing back and forth, back and forth, pointing and shouting. Sweat dotted his forehead. Anna recognized Brother Phil, the minister, from his Web picture.

They stood in the back for several seconds.

“Come on, Mom,” Anna whispered. “Let’s find a seat.”

Brother Phil paused and looked at them for the briefest of moments before he went back to his pacing and shouting.

The room was small and square and dismal. Rows of folding chairs faced the front. Brother Phil strode across a makeshift platform. The walls were unadorned. The whole room was rather plain.

A few people turned when they saw them enter and whispered behind their hands. Catherine's grasp on Anna's left arm increased as they made their way to the back row and took seats by the door.

Anna didn't know quite what she had expected, but she certainly thought more people would be attending than the dozen or so individuals scattered throughout the room. She looked at the man in front and wondered what his agenda was. And she contrasted this depressing gathering to the little white church in Whisper Lake Crossing that she had attended.

The lights in this room were glaring, yet there was a darkness about the place. The lamps that hung overhead cast strange shadows against the cement-block walls. The attendees almost seemed to be in a trance.

She didn't recognize any of the people who were sitting on the wooden chairs except for Lois and Marg. A man sat beside Marg. He wore a baseball cap and black glasses.

"Do you think we should go up and sit with Lois and Marg?" Catherine whispered to her.

Anna shook her head. "Let's stay here for now."

They did.

The preaching of this man could only be described as ranting. Anna tried to make sense of what he was saying and she couldn't. He was going on about evil, saying that it's right here in our midst, already in our midst. He ran down a litany of sins—adultery, immorality, heresy, filth. He said words whose definition Anna didn't even know. He emphasized each syllable with a pound of his fist.

What a contrast, she thought, to the message of love and grace in her church. She was learning in her own church that there was nothing she could do to make Jesus love her more, and there was nothing she could do to make Jesus love her less. Anna didn't know how she knew it, but she knew that the man up there now, this so-called Brother Phil, was poison.

As she listened, she found herself praying for Marg and for Lois. So intent was she on her conversation with God that she didn't notice that Stu had come in until he was sitting beside her.

Her breath caught. What was he doing here? She whispered that question to him.

"I followed you."

She whispered, "You've been following me around a lot lately."

"I like following you around," he whispered back. A man two rows ahead of them turned to look at the commotion. He frowned at them.

A few moments later she saw that Stu was not looking at Brother Phil. He seemed to be staring at the man next to Marg. He was frowning at him. Anna wondered why.

Finally, with a slap of fist against the pulpit,

Brother Phil was done. He raised one hand and prayed and Anna bowed respectfully, although by this time she sincerely doubted that this guy had any hotline to God at all.

Brother Phil made his way to the back of the church. When Marg and Lois stood up and saw Anna, Catherine and Stu, Marg's mouth formed a little O and Lois simply stared.

"What are you doing here?" Lois asked when she reached them at the back of the church.

"We heard you had special meetings and we decided we wanted to come to your, um, church. . . ." Anna choked on the word *church*.

Marg's eyes looked hollow as they flitted from one to the other and back again.

As soon as the service was over, Stu had made a beeline toward the man who had been sitting next to Marg. Catherine and Lois were in conversation, so that left her and Marg. Anna decided that she needed to encourage this woman. She knew firsthand how difficult it was to be with someone who was abusive, yet staying and staying even though you knew you should go. Even though Johnny might not be physically abusive, his philandering ways made him emotionally abusive to Marg, she was sure. Anna didn't know the precise circumstances, but she knew she wanted to reach out. She said to Marg, "If it's any help, Marg, I think I know what's going on. I know what's happening—"

But before she could finish, Marg made a choking sound like a gag. Her eyes got very big, she put a hand to her chest and slumped down into the nearest chair. Lois was there in an instant with her arm around the woman's shoulders and glaring up at Anna.

What had Anna said? What had she done? She was only trying to help.

Seeing the hyperventilating Marg, Brother Phil strode over to where Marg was still sitting on the chair. Lois's arm was around her and she was stroking the woman's back. By this time most of the others had gone, including the young man that Stu had talked with.

"Someone get her a paper bag!" Brother Phil shouted.

Marg bent her head low, and Anna couldn't help but wonder if these theatrics were a bit overdone. But then she remembered what Marlene had said, that Marg was afraid for her life. Or maybe the woman had really fallen ill. If that was the case, should they call an ambulance? She asked her mother about this.

"I don't know, dear," Catherine said. "I know she's been really upset about the bombing. Maybe this is just part of that. She's been through a lot."

Anna remembered what she'd been told about Marg, that she'd been thinking of leaving Johnny a long time ago, for adultery, one of the sins that brother Phil had railed against in his rant. Was that the reason she was so upset now? Anna also thought about Johnny being on the "list." Marg had probably seen this list. Maybe that's why she was so upset. Marlene said that Marg had been planning on leaving her husband, but perhaps she wasn't. Maybe they had worked things out now, and she was genuinely afraid for him.

It wasn't until Stu came over, squatted down to chair level in front of Marg and spoke softly that she perked up. Anna couldn't hear what they were talking about, but Marg nodded several times. She took Stu's hand and stood up.

At the end of it all, Anna introduced herself to Brother Phil as Lois's niece. She shook his chubby hand and said it was nice to meet him. He responded with, "Yes, yes." He seemed to be in a hurry to get away from her. He didn't look her in the eye, but focused somewhere over her shoulder and away from her.

Lois and Catherine helped Marg to the car and Stu turned to Anna. "Can we talk?" he asked.

"Okay."

"Can your mother get home without you? I can drive you home."

"I'm sure she can." He was standing close to her, looking down at her, and her heart was doing that thing again. Was he asking her out? No. Wanting to "talk" was not the same as going out on a date. *Stop thinking like that,* she told herself.

After Anna told her mother that she would be getting a ride home with Stu, she followed Stu to his vehicle. She looked at it in surprise. Then she looked at her arm with the cast. Stu's vehicle was a four-wheel quad.

"You drove that here?" she asked him.

"I'll help you get on."

"You had time to go home, get out of your car and get this?"

"I did. I went home, listened to a couple of phone messages and then decided to come along the beach to your place. I saw you getting into your mother's car, so I decided to follow you."

"I don't know how I'm going to get on this thing," Anna said.

"It has a pretty secure backrest. And I have an extra helmet. You'll be fine, I promise. Here, let me help you."

As he put the helmet on her and strapped it under her chin, his face was very close to hers. His expression was concentrated as he snapped the neck strap into place. That on, he took hold of her left elbow and helped her climb onto the backseat. Then he made sure she was okay.

Stu was right. The backseat of the quad felt secure. Then he wrapped a blanket around her.

"I have to check on something. That's why I drove in this. Then we'll head down the mountain. How about the Schooner Café to warm up with some coffee?"

She nodded. It sounded fine with her. She wrapped her left arm around him and it felt good.

"Hang on tight," Stu said.

They went up the Dragon Mountain Road until the road turned into a trail that was rough and full of ruts.

"Where are we going?" she asked.

"Just ahead a bit."

A few minutes later he stopped the quad, got off and examined something in the trees. It was getting dark and cold. Anna watched him and waited. He came back frowning, got on the quad and down they went to the Schooner Café.

They took a table far from the other patrons. He ordered coffee for himself and hot chocolate for Anna. There were few patrons in the Schooner Café at this time. Peach and Pete, two old men Anna had known all her life, were sitting in one corner working on a crossword puzzle together. A young mother with two children was in the center. There were some students and a few couples. That was about it.

"What were you checking up on the mountain?" she asked him.

"Oh." He shrugged. "Some kids were playing pranks up there. I had to see if they were up to their old tricks again."

She nodded, realized he probably had other police matters to deal with besides her case. "And were they?"

He shook his head. A waitress brought their drinks and set them on the table. Stu said, "So, what was all that with Marg back at the church?"

"I have no idea," Anna said, shrugging out of her coat. "I just told her that I thought I knew what she was going through and then she lost it. I was just trying to reach out to her. What did you say that calmed her down?"

"Not much." He stirred three packets of sugar and two creams into his coffee. "I just assured her that everything was going to be all right, that I live right behind her and anytime she had a problem she could come and see me."

"She seems to rely on you a lot," Anna said.

Stu shrugged. "A lot of people do." He smiled shyly at her and she felt her heart speed up.

She took a sip of her hot chocolate. She asked, "Who was that man you were talking to at the end of the service? I thought I saw you looking at him during Brother Phil's rant."

"*Rant*. That's a good word for it."

"So?" Anna cocked her head. "Why were you looking at him the way you were?"

"I thought he was someone I knew."

"And he wasn't?"

"I don't know. I didn't get his name. I looked over and Marg was in distress. By the time I calmed her down and looked back, the man was gone."

"I think he's Marg's boarder."

He nodded. “That’s who he is, all right. I saw his car there.”

“A silver car?” Anna asked.

“Right.”

He took a gulp of his very sweet coffee and said, “I got a message from Liz right before the service. They didn’t find any prints but yours on the cell phone, or the bell. But I’m not surprised at that. I wasn’t expecting any.”

“Someone is trying to frame me,” Anna said.

“I know. And I’m going to find out who.”

She looked down at her hot chocolate and said very quietly, “Thank you for believing me.”

He reached across the table and touched her left hand. The touch sent shivers through her body. She looked up and he was gazing at her intently. “During the last couple of weeks I’ve grown very fond of you, Anna. I know you had nothing to do with the bombing.”

“Thank you.” Anna felt a heat rise in her neck.

When they finished their drinks, they decided that Stu would drive her home along the beachfront in the quad.

“I could go get my car and drive you home,” he’d offered.

“No. This is fine. A ride along the beach will be nice.”

It was.

All too soon the ride was over. The stretch of beach was not very long and within minutes they were at the path that led up to the residential area where her mother lived. He shut down the four-wheeler and hopped off.

"That was fun," she said.

"When your arm is better and we can go longer distances, I'll take you all the way around Dragon Mountain. There's a trail there that's terrific."

"That would be great."

He helped her off the quad, then reached under her chin to undo the strap. Gently, he lifted the helmet off her head and laid it on the backseat. Then, he reached out, took her face into his hands and kissed her. He pulled her to him and held her that way for a long time.

As they broke apart and started up the trail to her mother's cottage, she wondered if she could trust him. She hoped so. But she was still afraid. She told him that.

"I believe you and I believe *in* you. You can trust me."

Just before they hit the residential sidewalk, he stopped.

"Anna," he said, suddenly serious. He put his arm around her waist, drew her to him and said quietly into her hair, "Just walk with me. Quickly."

"Stu?" She looked up at him.

"Just come quickly. Someone is following us. I'll tell you when we get to your mother's."

"Stu," she whispered. "You're scaring me."

"It's okay. I'm with you."

He held her very close to him as they walked fast to the front door of her mother's house. Inside, he said, "I heard something in the bushes. I just want you to be safe."

Catherine and Lois were home. While he carefully checked every door and window, he asked them how Marg was.

"We got her home okay. She's just a little shook up," Lois said.

"I think this whole thing with the bomb and Johnny is really frightening her," Catherine said. "I hope you find out who really did this."

"We're working on it," he said.

With Anna safely at home with her mother, Stu moved softly through a patch of woods bordering the lake. Whoever it was couldn't have gotten far. And whoever it was might hold the key to this entire case. Stu found no one.

But someone *had* been there. As he and Anna had walked up the path through the woods to her mother's house, he had heard the distinct sound of a person in the underbrush. And that person might still be here. He found a long stick on the ground and moved the brush aside. He was looking for anything that would prove that somebody had been following them. But, as on Dragon Mountain, there was nothing here. He kept looking with his flashlight, even though it was darker now.

He found his way back to the narrow path and headed down to his four-wheeler. Just as he was about to step onto the beach, he heard it again—that same quiet rustle in the brush. Was it the sound of a person lying low and trying not to be heard? Stu knew the woods. He'd grown up hunting with his father. He'd spent his boyhood in the woods. He knew the sounds that the woods made, and the sounds the woods did not make. This was not a sound the woods made.

He turned off his flashlight, looked in the direction from which the noise had come and took careful, measured steps toward it.

Then he heard it again. Someone was there! His senses keen, he stepped off the trail and into the underbrush. About ten yards away was a large fallen tree. Behind it would be the perfect hiding place. A person not wanting to be seen could crouch there and watch for hours. He crept closer.

Approximately ten feet away from the fallen log, he stopped and listened again. He heard the sounds faintly. He crept noiselessly closer.

At the last minute, he yelled, "Hey!"

He rounded the log in time to see two raccoons turn and run from where they had been playing.

If every nerve in his body hadn't been so tautly wound, this would almost have been funny.

He headed home on his quad. It was now fully dark. That settled it. He was losing it. He was tired. This case was taking its toll. He sighed.

He decided to stop in and see how Marg was doing. She answered the door wrapped in one of Johnny's robes and holding a mug of tea. It looked as if she had been crying.

"Are you okay, Marg? I just thought I'd stop in and see how you were doing. See if you needed anything."

"I'm okay. Thanks for coming by."

He said, "You had a bit of a scare at the church, didn't you?" He still didn't know what had frightened her so much. "Was it Anna who frightened you? Anna is just trying to be helpful. She cares a lot about you. She's worried about you."

"Why isn't she in jail, Stu? Wasn't she arrested?"

"She's been released to her mother's custody," Stu said.

"But she frightens me, Stu. That woman frightens me to death! I can't walk the streets knowing she's not behind bars."

"Don't be afraid of Anna, Marg. You have nothing to be afraid of."

She looked as if she was going to say something, then frowned and didn't.

Stu asked, "When does Johnny come home for good?"

"I'm not ready for him to come home. I have to have some ramps installed for the wheelchair and they were supposed to come and put the ramps in today, but they didn't come. While I was in church, they were supposed to be working on them, but nobody came."

"Maybe I could help," he said. "And what about your boarder? I met him at church and he seems like a nice guy. I'm sure he and I could work together and get those ramps in." Stu didn't know why he brought up the subject of her boarder. He had only talked to the man briefly. Yet there was something about the young man that struck Stu as strange.

She shook her head. "I couldn't ask him to help. He's only renting from me."

Stu asked, "I'm just curious. How did that guy come to be living here? Is he someone Johnny knows?"

She stared at him for several seconds before she shook her head. "He's just somebody from my church. Just someone who needed a place to stay."

And he drives a silver car that has followed me on more than one occasion, Stu thought. When he had seen that silver car at the church this evening he had made up his mind to talk to this man and find out just what his business in town was.

"I'm thinking of leaving him, you know," Marg said.

Stu looked up at her sharply. For one very weird moment he thought she was talking about her boarder.

She put her mug of tea down on the table by the

entrance and ran a hand through her hair. “I’m just trying to figure out if I should go now before he gets home. I’m talking about Johnny. He and Anna deserve each other.”

Stu stared at her. “What are you talking about?”

“Anna and Johnny. I know she has eyes for him. I can see it. And I’m thinking about not being here when Johnny finally comes home.”

“That’s ridiculous,” he said. “That’s just not true.” It was uncomfortable being in the middle of someone’s marriage problems. He didn’t want to take sides, yet he had seen Johnny with that woman in the pink suit. He remembered what Johnny had told him, how Marg had changed when she started going to that church. Still, that didn’t give Johnny an excuse to run around.

“I’m not so sure,” Marg said. “If you are looking at someone who might have wanted to kill my husband look at one of his many women. And you might want to begin with Anna. Everyone knows she did it. That’s why, when she came to me at my church, I was afraid.” She looked into his eyes. There were tears in hers. “I was afraid, Stu. When she walked over to me, I was afraid.”

He looked down at her. “Marg, she was just trying to help you. I know Anna, and you have nothing to be afraid of. Is your boarder in? I’d like to talk with him. I met him at the church, but we didn’t get a chance to finish our conversation.”

She looked up at him worriedly and said, “I

don't know. I didn't see him come home. Did you see his car?" She seemed agitated. "I don't know where he is, where he goes."

"I'll look," Stu said. "I'll try his door. Are you going to be okay?"

"If my doors are all locked, I'll be okay."

"You have my number. Call me if you need anything."

Before he left he made sure that all Marg's doors and windows were locked and that she was safe.

Then he knocked on the basement door. He felt his cell phone vibrate in his pocket, indicating a text message, so he pulled out the phone. It was from Steve. Call me when you can. I have some interesting information about the wire, the message said.

A few moments later the man he'd met that evening at church opened the door. He still wore his baseball cap, but his glasses were off. "Yes?"

"I wanted to talk to you earlier, but we were interrupted."

He scratched his nose. "Why did you want to talk with me?"

Stu edged himself into the room. He leaned his arm up against the door frame. "How do you know Marg and Johnny?"

The man shrugged. His face was pinched and his features sharp. "As I told you at church, I needed a place to live and Marg opened her home to me."

“Where are you from? Are you here on vacation?”

“Why the questions?”

“I’m just concerned about your landlady, Marg Seeley. I don’t like it when people take advantage of her.”

“No one’s taking advantage of her, believe me,” he said. “I was just about to go to bed. It’s been a long day for me.”

“Speaking of that, what do you do all day?”

“I’m looking for work here.”

“You’ve come to Whisper Lake Crossing looking for work? People who are looking for work leave Whisper Lake Crossing.”

He shrugged, and gave a bit of a smile. “What can I say? I like the lake.”

“What kind of work are you looking for?”

“Oh, anything . . .”

“I’m Stu McCabe, by the way,” he said. “I didn’t get your name.” He inched slowly into the man’s room. It was simply that—just one room besides a bathroom. In one corner was an unmade bed, next to that was a table with a laptop computer and along the opposite side, a small kitchenette with a sink. Clothes were scattered here and there. In short, the place was a mess. There were a series of hooks beside the door where the man had hung some sweaters and jackets, among them a couple of baseball caps and a bright red jacket. On the table, the man’s laptop was open. He'd been playing a game of Solitaire.

"That's because I didn't give it," he said. "Look, I'm a private person. I came here to get away. I came here to start over and look for a job. I don't know why you're bugging me. When I'm ready to come out and sit all day at the Schooner Café and talk to people, I'll let you know. But for now I just want to be left in peace."

Stu was not satisfied. Something was going on here. And for the life of him he couldn't figure out what it was.

Stu approached the man. "I'm with the sheriff's department," he said. "And I'd like to talk with you about your car."

The man looked at him wryly. "My car? What about my car? Do I have a parking ticket?"

"Nothing so simple as that. You were following me in your car and I want to know why."

"Following you? When? And why would I follow you? This is the first time I've ever seen you." The man stroked his chin and regarded Stu with a smirk. "I get it. You think I've got something to do with that bombing accident, don't you? I'm not from here and so you happen to see my car and right away I'm a suspect? Is that how it works up here in the north country? And following you? Let me tell you something. If I see a police car, I'm like every other car out there. I slow down." He opened his hands in a gesture of surrender. “You want to search my car? Be my guest. You’re not going to find anything.”

Stu had to reluctantly concede that the man had a point. No judge in the world would sign a search warrant on such flimsy evidence. Stu said, “If you hear anything, see anything, please call me.”

Stu dropped his business card on the man’s counter and left. He wasn’t satisfied, though. There was something about the man’s demeanor that just wasn’t sitting right with Stu. Call it gut feeling. Call it whatever you will, but on his way down to his cottage, he made a decision to keep an eye on Marg’s boarder.

TWELVE

Anna was having a frustrating day. She had just come home from the hospital and the news wasn't all that good. It looked as if her hand and wrist were going to require more surgery. Plus, a whole lot more physiotherapy after that. The doctor would know more in a couple of weeks. As she had sat in the hospital waiting to see the surgeon, she felt that everyone was looking at her. After all, she had been arrested for murder.

Lois and her mother were in Bangor for the day on a shopping bus tour, something they had signed up for long before any of this happened.

Stu had offered to come to the hospital with Anna, but she had declined.

"I'll be just fine," she had told him. "It's just routine. I'll be in and out."

She had told him about the appointment when he had called to tell her that the sound in the brush was nothing more than a pair of raccoons.

"There was no one following us in the brush. It was just some raccoons."

Her mother had made some coffee, and it was still in the coffeepot in the kitchen. She managed to pour some into a mug and then zap it in the microwave for a minute. It wouldn't be the best in the world, but it was too much work to make a fresh pot when she could only use one hand. She took it out to the front porch, set it on the wooden table and then went back inside for her Bible. She was getting used to carrying things one at a time.

Outside she sat down and was about to open to a passage in *Matthew* when she noticed the envelope. It was plain and white and legal-size, and it was leaning up against the porch railing. Was it something for her mother? Maybe it had dropped out of her mother's hands when she'd brought in the mail from the box out front.

She put her coffee down on a table and picked it up. It was addressed to her. And since there was no stamp on it she knew it hadn't been mailed. Someone had laid it here.

Maybe it was a get-well card. She'd received a number of these from people in the church.

She sat down on the porch swing and opened it up. Inside was one white sheet of paper. Centered on the page were the words, *HOW MUCH DO YOU WANT? DO NOT GO TO THE POLICE.*

She turned it over and frowned. Both the envelope and the note had been printed on a computer. It wasn't signed and there was no return address, so she had no idea who had dropped it off. She folded the paper back up and put it in the envelope. But she continued to be confused. How much did *who* want? She had no idea what it meant.

She pulled out her cell phone to call Stu when an unfamiliar car pulled into the driveway. Anna stuffed the envelope into her Bible and stood up. She smiled when she saw that it was Rodney. He was alone and grinning. He carried an enormous flowering plant.

"Hey, Anna," he said. "How are you doing?"

"Oh, um, I'm going to be trying out for Wimbledon tomorrow."

"Ha, ha. You're funny." He brought the plant up onto her porch and set it down. "I thought this plant might cheer you up."

"It does. Thank you, Rodney. Just seeing you cheers me up. I was at the hospital, and the news isn't all that good. I'll be in this contraption—" she lifted up her right hand "—for a bit longer than I anticipated." She told him what the doctor had said.

"Oh, Anna, that's too bad. But it won't be forever. You're talented and smart and you'll be back at the community college sooner than you think."

That was something Anna didn't even want to think about—her work. "There's a bit of cold coffee in the pot in the kitchen and a working microwave. But I can tell you for sure that the coffee is not all that good."

"How about if I make us a fresh pot? Dump that stuff out. I can smell it from here. It's burned."

They went inside and she sat down at a kitchen table while he set about washing out the coffeepot, grinding some beans and starting a new pot. It occurred to her that she'd left her Bible outside with the letter inside. She'd have to remember to pick it up later. For now, though, it was nice to have a familiar face, one of her favorite students, here for a visit. The brewing coffee did smell good.

Rodney found two mugs in her mother's cupboard and set them on the table while he told her that a special scholarship was being established in Claire's and Hilary's names. Already almost a thousand dollars had been donated.

Anna was pleased. They chatted about that for a while. Rodney and Claire's sister, Lily, had been instrumental in setting it up. He poured cream into his coffee and looked at her across the table. "So when *do* you think you'll be back teaching?"

"I don't know if I'll ever be able to."

He looked at her dumbfounded. "Of course you will. You're a great teacher, Anna, and you can still teach. You're our teacher and in Hollywood you had such fantastic experience. You teach with your head not your hands. The artistry is not in your fingers—it's in your head."

She reached over and touched his arm with her left hand. "You're so sweet to be telling me this."

"Well, it's true, Anna. I'm so sorry you had to go to the hospital by yourself. You should have called. I would have come. Isn't your mother here? I saw her earlier."

"You couldn't have. She and my aunt have been in Bangor since the wee hours."

"Maybe it wasn't your mother, then. I saw a woman on your porch—I just assumed it was your mother. There was a guy with her, too. Before I got partway up the walk the guy yelled to me that if I was coming to see you, you weren't here."

Anna stopped and looked at him. "You saw two people on this front porch? Here? What did they look like?"

"I didn't get a really good look."

"But you saw people on my porch?"

He told her that the man looked to be in his mid-thirties, and the woman was hidden behind the wind chimes, so he really didn't see her at all. He just assumed it was Anna's mother, but she didn't speak.

Anna cupped her hand around the coffee mug, and tried to maintain her self-control. Someone was on her porch and this was the someone who could have put that note here.

"Have the police figured out who Hilary was afraid of?" Rodney asked.

She shook her head. "Not that I know of."

Rodney frowned. "I just keep thinking about her, ya know? Did you know she filed a restraining order against her husband? I know she was afraid of him."

"I didn't even know she'd been married until recently."

"Lily, Claire's sister, told me about the restraining order. It was something she just remembered."

"I wish I had known all this about Hilary. It would have helped me to understand her better. I just feel so bad about both Hilary and Claire. Sometimes I'm just overcome with sadness."

"I know what you mean."

By the time they finished their coffee it was late afternoon.

After Rodney left, Anna called Stu, but got his voice mail, so she turned on the porch light and sat on the porch swing. She retrieved her Bible from the porch and pulled out and read the note again. She still couldn't understand what it meant. She put it back in the envelope and back into her Bible, and put the Bible on her nightstand. She felt antsy and sad. She was also surprised that Stu hadn't been there to answer his phone. He was probably busy. There were a lot of things going on.

She decided to try out the parlor's new reading nook for the first time. Anna picked up her novel in her left hand and flicked the reading nook light switch with the hard surface of her cast.

She felt a jolt go through her body, saw a flash of light and smelled something acrid and sharp, like burning electrical wires. She felt herself flung toward the bed, where she landed with a thud, half on and half off, and blacked out.

"Anna!"

Anna opened her eyes. "Wha . . . ?" She shaded her eyes with her left hand. Someone was shining what looked like a flashlight in her eyes.

"Anna!" She recognized her mother's voice. "Are you okay? The electricity's off. And what are you doing with your head hanging over the edge of the bed like that?"

"Mom, um, I . . ." Her head hurt. She tried to get up. "What am I doing like this?"

Her mother helped to lift her back onto the bed. "You're in the parlor. Lois and I just got home, and all the lights were off. . . ."

"I turned the porch light on for you. I distinctly remember. . . . Did the power go off?"

"It must have. When we got home there wasn't a light on in the house."

Anna sat up and put her legs over the edge of the bed. She rubbed her temple with her left hand. Her right arm ached in a way it hadn't for a while. Also, the fingers of both hands tingled. Her head hurt, but that could have been from hanging over the side of the bed.

Lois asked, "Are you okay? You're not misusing your pain pills are you, Anna?"

Anna shot her a look. She didn't like her aunt's insinuations. She was fully upright now. "I wish I knew what happened."

"Uh-oh," Lois said. She was aiming a flashlight at an electrical switch plate on the wall of her room. The wallboard around the switch plate was blackened. "Does this have something to do with why the electricity is off?"

Catherine took a look at it. Then Anna remembered. She had hit the light switch to the reading nook with her cast, and the next thing she knew she was lying on the bed, half on and half off. She told her mother and aunt this.

Catherine said, "Oh, dear. It must have been a faulty switch and now the electricity's off in the whole house."

Anna said she felt dazed. The bones of her legs hurt.

"You were shocked!" Catherine said, rushing toward her. "You touched that and you got an electrical shock."

"Maybe."

"We're going to take you to the hospital," her mother said.

"Must have been a short," Lois said. "And we just had all this rewired. This should not have happened. You said you turned on the light switch with your cast?"

"I was holding my novel in the other hand. So I sort of leaned into it with my right arm. I thought for once that I would actually try doing two things at the same time."

"Let's have a look at that cast," Catherine said.

They did. The place on the cast where she had leaned into the light switch was blackened and burned like the wall.

Catherine said, "That fiberglass cast may have saved your life. But you should go to the hospital anyway. I'm calling Stu."

Anna didn't complain. She held weakly on to her mother's arm as they made their way to the car.

Stu met Anna, Catherine and Lois at the hospital. By the time he got there, they had found Anna a bed and the doctor had been called in. They ran some tests, but everything looked normal. Still, they wanted to keep her overnight.

Stu told them that Alec and Steve planned to go over every inch of the wiring in the house. They were already there.

"I'm sure it's something with the old wiring," Catherine complained to Stu. "The electrician said they were going to replace all of it. They must have missed something."

Anna listened as Catherine gave Stu the names and numbers of the electrician she'd hired. "I'm so sorry," Catherine said to her.

"Don't be sorry," Anna said, reaching out for her mother.

"It's not your fault," Stu said. "We'll find out if this was deliberate."

When Stu got to Catherine's house, Alec and Marlene's husband, Roy, were already there. Lanky Roy had his long legs wrapped around a low hassock on the parlor floor. He was examining the offending electrical box with his long, knobby fingers. He wore latex gloves, Stu noticed. They would probably be sending this switchbox to the forensics lab to be thoroughly examined. Stu knew that process could take months. Roy, however, would be able to give them a good preliminary evaluation.

Roy looked up when Stu arrived. "I wish Catherine had called me to this install this. Who did she get? Do you know?"

Stu said he didn't know.

"It's all wrong. It's totally backward. We've got the ground wire hooked in with a positive that should be a negative, and the negative's just hanging loose. No wonder it all shorted out. In fact, it was wired to send the electric current to the metal box as soon as you threw the switch. That means the little screws on the switch cover would be a full 120 volts. I told Alec we need to look at every electrical box in this house."

"That's a good idea. Do you think somebody jimmied this particular one?" Stu asked.

Roy shook his head. "Hard to say. But it sure

looks like it. They'd have to know what they were doing, though. I mean, it takes just as much electrical know-how to get a light switch to short out like this as it does to put one in properly."

Alec was scrutinizing the blackened wallboard. He said, "Steve is coming. I'd like his take on things, as well. There's something going on, and we need to get to the bottom of it."

Stu heartily agreed.

Alec went on, "Steve is meticulous. I hope you don't have anything planned for tonight, Stu. Because I think it's going to be a long night. If I know Steve, he's going to want to go over this entire house with a fine-tooth comb."

"Fine with me." If this would finally prove that Anna had nothing to do with the City Hall bombing, then it was worth it. But was this connected to the bombing at all? How did the pieces fit together?

"We're going to be here for a long time, so I think the ladies are going to have to find another place to stay for the time being," Alec said.

"I'll call Bette," Stu said.

"I was thinking of Steve and Nori's place at Trail's End, but Flower Cottage would even be better. It's closer to everything."

When Stu called Bette, she was more than willing to open up her home. In addition, Stu and Alec decided to stay there, too, along with Alec's wife, Megan. Bette had plenty of rooms and it would be good to have a couple of officers there. She had no other guests at the moment.

While they waited, Stu called Anna on her cell phone and told her about the overnight arrangements for her mother and aunt. “I’ll be going over there, too. Alec and I have both decided to stay at the house, so there will be police officers there.”

“Stu, there’s something I need to do. I got a letter. It’s in an envelope in my Bible and my Bible is on the nightstand in my room. Can you get it for me?” Anna asked.

“It must be an important letter,” he said.

“Can you get it without showing it to any of the other police who are there? It’s a very private letter. I’ll let you read it when you bring it to me later tonight or tomorrow.”

Stu said he would.

He easily found the letter in Anna’s Bible. Because she had asked him not to show it to anyone, he put it in a pocket inside his jacket.

When Steve finally arrived, he immediately took control. He asked the right questions and gave the right assignments. While Alec and Roy systematically looked through the electrical boxes, he pulled an envelope out of his pocket and handed it to Stu.

“I got a lot of information on that wire in the woods. I wrote it all down.”

Stu took out the sheet and skimmed it. He looked up at Steve. “Marine wire?” he said.

"Used in marine applications. This particular wire came from an old sailboat. It's been weathered and we found salt corrosion in it. It's probably from an old sailboat that spent a lot of time on the ocean."

"So not a boat that would be on Whisper Lake?"

"There's salt in the strands of the wire. This is a small lake and the water isn't salty. That wire was on a sailboat that spent most of its time on the ocean."

Stu, who knew nothing about sailboats, asked, "What do they use that wire for?"

"For sailboat rigging. Either standing rigging or running rigging."

So it came from a boat. Another piece of the puzzle to add to the mix. And he was being taken right back to the beginning. Hilary's ex-husband was currently sailing up the coast. Connection? He didn't know, but it was worth pursuing. He just didn't know how. He put Steve's report in his pocket next to Anna's letter and called Liz. He decided he wanted someone to come to the hospital and stay with Anna all night. He was remembering the dream she had about being smothered and remembering the man he had seen on the elevator.

When he finally got hold of Liz, she told him she had tracked down the license-plate number of the silver car.

"Tell me," he said.

"It's stolen."

The wire strung across the path, the faulty electrical box, the bombing and now a stolen silver car. He was sure they were getting closer to figuring it all out. And the first thing they had to do was bring in Marg's boarder for questioning.

THIRTEEN

Anna was glad that Sara was the night nurse again.

"You again," Sara said, but she was smiling.

"Yep. Me again. Can't get rid of me that easily."

Sara stopped, stood at the end of her bed. "You seem sad. Are you okay? How's the head?"

"I feel okay physically. Maybe a little tired. There are going to be police checking on me all night."

Sara nodded. "We know all about that. Right now there's a guard sitting outside your door—did you know that? I admit that this is a first for us in Whisper Lake Crossing Hospital. Now, can I get you something? Toast? Juice?"

"I don't think I could eat anything."

"Well, if there's anything, anything at all, just give me a buzz. I'll be in later to take your temperature and all those other lovely things."

A couple of hours later, Liz came and sat down on a chair in the corner. Stu had told Anna that Liz would be staying with her for the night. Anna said, "Hello."

"Hi. I'll be here for a while. Also, if I were you I wouldn't talk. There are still those charges pending."

Liz seemed agitated. Maybe it had something to do with where she'd just been. Even though she sat in an uncomfortable, straight-back chair, she pulled one leg up and under her and opened a book. Anna didn't sleep. Occasionally she looked over at Liz, who had affixed one of those little book lights to her book.

"You have a hard and interesting job," Anna said out loud a short time later. "The pieces have to fit together to form the whole."

Liz looked up from her book. "What?"

"I just said you have a difficult job. I admire you."

"Thanks. I enjoy it."

"I can tell.

"I come from a family of police officers. My father was a policeman."

"I can't imagine it."

Liz got up. "I'm going for a cup of coffee. You want one? The guard is in the hall. I'll be back in ten minutes."

"No, thank you," Anna said.

She couldn't sleep. She thought about her arrest. She thought about her arm, and that gave way to thinking about her job. How would she work if she only had limited use of her hand? "The artistry is in your head, not your fingers," she could almost hear Rodney say.

As she pondered that and prayed, she thought that perhaps it was true. Perhaps God had something new in store for her, something exciting for her to do, someone new to be.

She heard a bit of a commotion and looked up to see a doctor standing in her doorway, leaning into the doorjamb and pushing buttons on a cell phone with his thumbs. She lay very still and watched him. She looked over to where Liz had been. The security guard was not there, either. Neither was Stu. Where were they?

Anna didn't move. The doctor was looking at her, but she was sure that in the darkness he thought she was sleeping. Without moving her head, she looked for the call button. Nowhere in sight. Slowly, Anna moved her left hand, searching for the nurse call button. The doctor looked as if he just come from surgery. He was wearing green scrubs and, again, a surgical mask.

Anna was suddenly very frightened. It came to her all at once that this was the man who had tried to smother her with a pillow when she was first brought in after the bombing! Should she call out? But the guards had all disappeared.

She moved her left hand slowly to feel for that call button. It had fallen down along the side of the bed. She found the end of the cord and gradually began bringing it up beside her.

When she found the button, she pressed it over and over again. At the same time she sat up quickly and yelled as loud as she could, "Sara!"

Anna heard running in the hallway. Sara appeared in her room. "What?"

"He was here. The man who tried to kill me. He was standing at the door," Anna said.

"What man?"

"The man. The doctor. He was in the doorway. Who was he? He was here before."

She said, "There's no doctor here, Anna. No one is here."

Anna knew what she had seen. This time it couldn't be blamed on medication.

Anna said, "I saw him. Where were you, Sara, just a moment ago? Maybe five minutes? Were you at the nurses' station?"

"I was checking on a patient."

"Are there any other nurses? How many are on duty tonight?"

"This is a small hospital. We only have two tonight. But we got a couple of nursing calls just a minute ago. So both of us were checking on patients . . ." She stopped and put a hand to her mouth. "But it was the strangest thing. When we got to the rooms our patients had fallen back to sleep."

Liz came back into the room, holding a coffee. She saw Sara and said, "What happened?"

They told her. Then Anna said quietly, "Sara, think back, remember back to when I was here that first week—when I said that someone tried to smother me."

"I remember," Sara said. Something seemed to dawn on her. "It was the same then. Someone down the opposite hall rang the nursing bell. I went, but the patient was asleep by the time I got there."

"Then he's here!" Liz said. "Whoever he is, he's still here." She pulled out her cell phone and Sara rushed to call security to secure the exits.

"We'll get him this time," Liz said to Anna. "He couldn't have gotten away."

But Anna wasn't so sure.

Alec was right. This was turning out to be a night of no sleep. As soon as Liz told Stu about the license number, the two of them had gone together out to the Seeley mansion to talk to the basement dweller.

"I did some research on the car's owner," Liz had told Stu on the way over. "The car is registered to a Mr. Reginald Pinter. He didn't answer his phone—that's why it took me so long to track this thing down. I did some more digging. Through his neighbors I was able to find out where he was. Reginald Pinter, who lives in Naples, Massachusetts, is currently overseas on business. Two weeks ago he left his car in long-term parking at Logan Airport. I gave him the bad news about his stolen car. He'll be on his way home tomorrow."

"So," Stu said when he had parked the squad car in the Seeleys' circular driveway. "Marg's boarder steals a car from long-term parking. That way it doesn't get reported stolen for a while. Good thinking. He gets a car and comes out here long enough to bomb City Hall. I should have paid more attention to him. I should have listened to my gut instinct. The moment I saw him I knew there was something off about him. I don't see the silver car here, do you?"

"Nope," Liz said. "Unless he parked around back somewhere. I guess we'll soon find out."

Flashlights in hand, they made their way around the side of the Seeley mansion. There were a few lights on in the main part of the house, but they weren't interested in the main part of the house; they were interested in the basement apartment. The basement was dark.

Stu knocked. No answer. Stu banged louder and called, "Police! Open up! Now!"

Still no answer. The place remained in darkness.

"What do you think?" Liz asked. "He could be a heavy sleeper."

"Or he could be gone."

Instead of trying to break down the door, they decided to talk to Marg. She must have seen or heard them, because as soon as they walked up her front steps she was on the porch.

"Stu?" she said, looking from one to the other and back again. Her lower lip quivered.

"Marg," Stu said. "We're looking for the man who stayed in your basement."

Marg didn't say anything for a while. She

twisted her hands in front of her. She didn't look at them, but looked at a spot over their shoulders when she said, "He's gone. He left today."

"What do you mean gone?" Liz asked.

"He moved out."

"Marg," Stu said. "Who was he and what was he doing in Whisper Lake Crossing? It's time you told us everything you know about him, and how he came to live here."

"I told you. I met him in church."

"Marg." Stu softened his voice. "What is his name? Please. No tricks. We need his name."

Her lip quivering, she said, "I didn't know him too well. Just from church. His name is Reg, Reg Pinter. That's all I know. I just know his name."

"How did you know him from church?"

Marg put a shaky hand to her face. "We just . . . got an announcement . . . in church . . . that someone needed a place to stay." She spoke each word slowly. "So . . . I . . ." She stopped. "Did he do something wrong? Is that why the two of you are here?"

Liz said, "The car he drove was stolen, and we also don't believe that the name of the person who stayed here was Reginald Pinter. The real Reginald Pinter is in England and is flying home tomorrow."

"Oh, dear." Marg looked near tears.

"We need to see his apartment."

Marg nodded, went inside. "I'll have to find the

key," she said. "I don't know where it is." She put a hand to her face. "I think it's upstairs. Wait in the foyer. I'll be right down with the key."

As soon as Marg went up her long staircase, Stu walked right through the foyer.

"Where are you going?" Liz whispered as Stu made his way down the hallway toward the kitchen.

He motioned her to follow him. Marg's laptop was closed on the kitchen table. Stu lifted the lid and sat down in front of it.

"You shouldn't be doing that," Liz said.

Stu ignored Liz. He was staring down to the last Web page that had been opened on her computer. It was a bomb-making Web site. "Take a gander at this." He made no attempt to keep his voice down.

"Interesting," Liz said.

Marg came back with the key and stood in the doorway looking at them, a shocked expression on her face.

"Interesting Web site you're looking at, Marg."

"Do you know you can find practically anything on the Web?" Marg seemed calmer than she was before. "I was going to talk to you about that. I was just seeing how easy it was to find information like this on the Internet. It's really easy. Did you know how easy it is?"

"I know," Stu said.

"I was doing this because I was thinking about

my Johnny. He was almost killed by a bomb. Anyone could have done that to my Johnny."

"Speaking of your Johnny," Stu said. "I saw him tonight. He says he would love to have you come and visit him."

Marg walked over and closed the lid of her computer. "I haven't been able to get up there and visit him yet. I'm a bit shaky in my car."

"Right," Stu said. "Do you have that key to the apartment?"

She handed it to him. "And I am amazed," she said, shaking her head, "at how easy it would be for someone just to follow the directions online to make a bomb. I'm horrified, actually."

The three of them went into the basement apartment. It was no surprise to Stu that the entire room was clean. The computer and printer were gone. The dishes in the sink were washed and put away. Stu smelled bleach. Whoever had lived here had packed up, cleaned up and gone. Stu wandered around the empty apartment. He had no doubt that there would be no trace of fingerprints, nothing. Yes, this man had cleaned up after himself well. Stu was fairly confident that they wouldn't find a usable fingerprint in the entire apartment, but that didn't mean they weren't going to try.

After he dropped Liz off at the hospital, he brought Alec up-to-date. Alec and Steve were still going through the electrical wiring at

Catherine's house, but it was looking more and more as if this was the only switchbox that had been tampered with. They should bring the Shawnigan and DeLorme police in to help them with this. It was clear that they had more on their plate than their three-person department could handle.

Alec told Stu to go home. He and Steve and the squad from DeLorme would be dusting Marg's basement apartment for fingerprints.

Stu went home, but not to sleep. How could he sleep? Instead, he sat on the couch in his living room and pulled out Anna's letter, fingered it bit, considering, but didn't open it. He put it back in his jacket pocket.

Next he went over Steve's report in full. The wire came from the rigging of an old sailboat. It suddenly came back to him. Hilary's ex-husband was sailing up the coast right now. On a sailboat. Connection? Possibly. Stu didn't know. He got out his notebook, found the cell-phone number for Hilary's ex-husband, Jack. He phoned him, even though it was the middle of the night. A message informed him that the party he was trying to reach was out of range.

He had begun making notes, drawing lines, creating a chart.

That's when he must have dozed, because at a little after three in the morning, his phone rang, jarring him out of a deep sleep.

It was Liz. Something was happening at the hospital. Something with Anna.

He grabbed his jacket and his gun, hoping for the best but expecting the worst.

FOURTEEN

They searched the entire hospital, every broom closet, every patient room. They found no one. The man in the green scrubs was not there. Whisper Lake Crossing Hospital wasn't large. It didn't take Stu, Alec, the nurses and the hospital security guards very long to go through every floor.

Stu found the pile of wrinkled green scrubs behind a chair near the loading-dock entrance. It was out back—an easy area to escape undetected.

Stu called Alec over. "Look at this," he said, lifting up each item of clothing with the end of his pen. There were booties, pants, a shirt, mask and cap. Stu said, "I'll bag them. There could be DNA, hair, something we can find."

Alec bent down, looked through the items one by one and frowned. "My thinking is that he's not going to even be in the police system. If he was, he wouldn't have left these here. He'd be more careful."

Stu was thinking. "If he's not in the system, if he's never been arrested before, then this is his first time. So this isn't a random thing. This is personal. He's taunting us."

Alec said, "My money is still on the missing-in-action Peter Remington."

Stu frowned. "I'm not so sure. If he's the same guy who was at that church, Anna would have instantly recognized him. She didn't."

"What about disguises?"

"Not impossible, but I still think Anna would have recognized something. She knew the guy very well, and she's a makeup artist, so she would be able to see through a disguise."

Stu went up to Anna's room. She would probably be sleeping. He just wanted to look in on her. Liz would stay in her room. Steve was even going to stay the night at the hospital, and of course everyone who was working there was on high alert.

Anna was awake when Stu came to the doorway. She gave him a weak, "Hi." Liz was there, too. When Stu entered, Liz said, "Do I have time to run down and get a cup of coffee? Mine got spilled when all the commotion began."

"Go on," he said.

"I won't be a minute."

"Take all the time you need."

He pulled up a chair and sat close to Anna. The back of her bed was in the upright position. She looked tired. There were dark circles under her eyes, yet to him, she still looked beautiful. "I'm so sorry to cause so much trouble," she said.

"You're no trouble," Stu said. "You're never trouble." As he sat beside her bed at three-thirty in the morning he knew beyond a doubt that he loved her. And as big a surprise as this was to Stu, it was a very pleasant surprise.

He didn't quite believe it was happening to him. When his beloved wife, Alesha, died, he never thought he would love again. Alesha was beautiful and strong, and she loved what he loved—mountain-biking, hiking, skiing. She had been a helicopter pilot in the military on her last deployment in Iraq. They were going to start a family when she got home.

She never made it. Instead, the transport vehicle she was riding in the back of, designed to look like an ordinary cement truck, was blown up near Baghdad.

To get away from Boston and all the reminders of Alesha, he had taken this job way out here in the three-person Whisper Lake Crossing Sheriff's Department. What he planned to do was to fill his life with the backcountry and the out of doors. He never expected to fall in love. In fact, he vowed he wouldn't.

Now, as he looked at Anna's sweet smile, he thought how different she was from Alesha. His outgoing, freckle-faced Alesha didn't even know what makeup was. Now he found himself falling for someone who applied it for a living.

The magazine on her tray featured home-interior designs. He looked down at it and said, "The man who was in the green scrubs isn't here anymore."

"That first night when I was here, it really was someone trying to smother me, wasn't it?"

"We think so. Maybe." He didn't want to frighten her, but he did want her to recognize that she was in real danger.

"Did you bring my letter?" she asked.

He patted his jacket.

"Did you read it?" she asked.

"You asked me not to. I didn't."

She gave him a shy smile. "You could have, though. Read it now. It's important, but I can't figure it out."

He took it out of his pocket and laid it on her tray table. She reached for it with her left hand, tried to open it. "It takes me a while to do anything one-handed. Why don't you do the honors?"

He pulled out the sheet of paper and laid it down on the table. He looked at it, puzzled. "What is it?" he asked.

"This was leaning up against my porch earlier today. It was addressed to me, but I can't figure out who it's from or what they want."

She told him that Rodney had come for a visit, and remarked that two people were on her porch. Stu looked at her intensely. Maybe he needed to talk with Rodney again. "I don't know what will happen to me now that I've showed this to the police. The letter said not to show this to the police. It sounded like a threat."

"We'll deal with that. Don't worry about it. And, Anna, thanks for trusting me."

"It's hard for me to trust anyone."

"I know."

"But I'm getting better at it. I'm learning."

"I hope I'm a good teacher."

Before he left, he bent down, gave her a soft kiss and vowed within himself that he would never let anything bad happen to her again.

He only hoped he could keep his promise.

Stu didn't see Anna until the following evening. He had spent the day trying to track down Peter Remington, Jack Habrowser and Reginald Pinter; talking to marine stores about halyard wire; and following up with Alec, Steve and Roy on the electrical box at Catherine's house, the fingerprinting crew at the Seeleys' basement apartment and the letter that Anna had received.

All day long he wanted to stop in and see Anna, but he barely had time to phone her. He knew, though, that he would be seeing her this evening. All of them would be together. All of them would be staying at Flower Cottage, except for Lois, who elected to stay with Marg at the Seeley mansion.

That was fine with Stu. He was also worried about Marg's safety and had invited her to Flower Cottage, but she declined. Should Stu believe Marg's story that she was just looking up bomb-making sites out of sheer curiosity? Or was there a more sinister reason behind her Web surfing?

By the time he got to Flower Cottage, a cold rain was falling. The warm sunshine of just a week ago had shifted into this harbinger of winter. The sky spat down frigid, unrelenting rain. Bette had supper going when he entered the kitchen—a thick chicken soup for all of them. Bette was at the counter chopping salad veggies while Catherine was getting plates down from the cupboard. Anna was sitting at the table, her hand around a mug of coffee. She smiled up at him when he entered, but she seemed unsure, maybe afraid. He knew she had reason to be.

They all welcomed him and Stu said, "Wow, something smells good. I think I'm going to like this hotel."

If the circumstances for everyone's stay hadn't been so serious, the mood at Flower Cottage could have been described as almost festive. Anna and her mother had decided to share a room on the second floor overlooking the lake and Alec and Megan chose a room opposite that one and down the hall. Liz opted for the small bedroom at the top of the stairs, right next to Bette's spacious room. Ralph, Bette's son, had the loft in the attic. Stu would stay on the main floor in the room off the one Bette called the library.

"Coffee?" Bette asked.

"Sure. Let me wash up and I'd love some."

"Caf, or decaf?"

"High test," Stu said. "Definitely high test."

He went into the room that would be his and dumped his duffel bag in a small room on the main floor.

When he had changed out of his uniform, he came out and sat beside Anna. "How are you feeling?" he asked quietly.

"Better," she told him quietly. "They did a bunch of tests and nothing's wrong with me. But I got this." She pulled out her cell phone, laid it on the table and pressed some of the buttons. "It's so awkward to do this with one hand."

Catherine and Bette were talking at the counter and couldn't hear this conversation. That was obviously the way Anna wanted it.

"This text message," she said handing him her cell phone. Her hand was shaking.

Stu took the phone from her and read:

I asked you how much you wanted. We are prepared to pay. But if you don't get back to us, other people will die.

Stu stared down at it. Then up at Anna. "No caller ID?"

"It's blocked."

Stu said, "Can I borrow your phone for a bit?"

She nodded. There were tears in her eyes. "I just wish I knew what it meant. *What* other people are going to die? And why?"

• • •

It was late at night. Everyone else had gone to bed long ago. Anna, who was not able to sleep, had wandered downstairs to the kitchen. She was standing by the window now, watching the full moon and thinking.

On one end of the large pine kitchen table beside her, a jigsaw puzzle lay partially completed. Earlier, Bette's son, Ralph, had gotten out the various boxes of jigsaw puzzles from the cupboard and together they chose one that featured a lighthouse surrounded by a garden. Ralph and Catherine and Alec's wife, Megan, had spent most of the evening drinking hot cocoa and working on it, piece by piece.

Anna hadn't. She had merely watched. Neither had Stu. Or Alec or Liz. Stu had Alec spread the case notes all over the coffee table in the living room while Liz was on the phone. Anna knew they were still trying to find Peter. Had Peter sent her those messages? But why? It made no sense.

Anna felt tired, and yawned several times, but she knew she wouldn't sleep. When everyone else went to bed so did Anna, but she tossed and turned, and couldn't find a comfortable position for her arm. Then she remembered that she had left the last of the pain pills in the parlor at her mother's house. So when sleep wouldn't come, she got up, went downstairs and now stood by herself at the window and looked out at the blackness of Whisper Lake. It was cool in the kitchen and she clutched an afghan around her shoulders. Outside, it looked cold, windy and blustery.

A part of her felt fear, but another part of her just felt numb. It was as if her entire life was in a holding pattern. It was as if she was waiting for something important, something from God. As she stood there at the open window she thought of the verse in Isaiah. *They who wait upon the Lord will renew their strength. They will rise up with wings like eagles. They will run and not be weary. They will walk and not faint.*

That was her—waiting. Waiting to see what kind of feelings developed for Stu. Waiting to see what kind of mobility she would end up having in her right hand. Even waiting to remember what exactly had happened when she entered City Hall on that fateful day. And here she was, not even in her own place. Waiting. That's all she seemed to be doing lately. Waiting to see what happened with her arrest. Alec said that they were going to drop the charges against her; they'd just been overwhelmed with work. She said she understood.

She was formulating a theory, a scenario. When she had lain awake in the hospital last night, she had dreamed a dream she couldn't remember. She had awakened with a start. It was after that that she began coming up with the picture. But the letter and text message were confusing to her. How did they fit in?

A red leaf blew up against the window for a moment, lay flat against the pane as if trying to gain entrance. Then, just as quickly, another gust blew it away.

She watched that same red leaf dance across the black lawn in the moonlight. Stu and Alec were looking for Peter. She knew that. But she wasn't sure Peter was responsible anymore. In fact, she was quite sure he wasn't.

A cloud scudded across the moon and her thoughts went back to the day of the bombing. She had thought the man in the red jacket, the one who'd looked over at her at that moment, was Peter. She had thought that the man she had seen talking to that woman, holding something away from her grasp, was Peter.

She gasped audibly. Red jacket! Where had that memory suddenly surfaced from? She put a hand to her mouth. He was wearing a red jacket. Bright red. Too red. Not something Peter would wear. It wasn't Peter!

Think, she said to herself. There had been something in the corner of her eye just before she went into City Hall that day. She'd been holding her very full cardboard cup of coffee. She had added too much cream to the top, and even with the plastic lid, it was leaking over the sides. She had been holding it away from her body, and trying to ignore Johnny. She hated the way he leered at her.

Just before she had gone into the building, she had looked to the right, for the briefest of instants. What had she seen? There had been someone there. A red jacket. Someone in a bright red jacket was talking to a woman. The woman was shorter than the man. Or was it a woman? Maybe not. Maybe it was a short man.

At the time she'd thought it was Peter. That's what she remembered, that Peter had come back. But no. The man she had seen in the red jacket was not Peter.

Anna let out a little gasp. She stared ahead of her at the moon. Was the woman Marg? She let those thoughts settle for a while.

So intent was she on her train of thought that Anna didn't hear the footsteps behind her.

The arms that went around her pulled her back away from the window.

"You need to get away from the window, Anna." He held on to her with one hand and with the other he pulled the curtains closed. "These should be kept closed."

She turned. It was Stu who was behind her. She went into his arms. He drew her to him and kissed her.

When they finally pulled apart, she said, "There was a red jacket."

"What?"

"A red jacket. And a person beside him. And they were holding something. He was trying to keep whatever it was away from her and they were arguing."

"What, Anna?"

"I saw him when I was walking into City Hall with my coffee. I remembered. I just remembered."

His arm was still around her waist, but his face wore a puzzled expression. They sat down at the table in the dining room and talked.

Anna wrote the name *Hilary* on a piece of paper. And next to it she wrote one word—*fear.* What she had seen on the young woman's face in her classroom was not anger or confusion, but fear. And then there was Hilary's sister saying that her sister was so afraid that she'd gotten a restraining order against her ex-husband. Hilary's mother had been so afraid that she didn't even mention Hilary's ex-husband when the police first questioned her.

Underneath the name *Hilary,* she wrote the name *Marg*. By her own admission, Marg was self-taught at the computer.

Then there was the red jacket, the text messages, the letter, the windowpane, the halyard wire and myriad other threats, including the light switch that had been tampered with.

It was all making sense now. It was all fitting together. At the end, they had it all figured out. Or thought they did.

• • •

Anna chose her time carefully. Catherine called Lois to help clean up the house after the police were finally finished with it and that left Marg alone in the mansion.

Anna knew this when she climbed up the front steps and rang the doorbell. "Can I come in, Marg?" she asked when the door was opened.

"Yes," Marg said.

Anna followed. When Marg stopped in the foyer, Anna walked past her and into the kitchen; Marg had no choice but to follow. Anna sat down on one of Marg's kitchen chairs. Marg sat across from her. The woman seemed unnaturally calm, yet the pinky finger on her right hand quivered slightly, betraying her nervousness.

Anna said, "I got your text message and I'm here to talk terms."

"You didn't respond to my letter."

"I didn't respond because I ended up in the hospital after almost being electrocuted, as you will no doubt remember."

Marg smiled, clasped her hands tightly to hide her shakiness. It was Anna's guess that Marg had never engaged in any sort of blackmail before. If this was new to Marg, it was also very new to Anna. Anna knew she needed to hold her own, stand her ground. It was important for her to get certain questions answered, for her own benefit. She had almost died in that bombing and Marg owed her some answers.

Anna proceeded. "Can you answer just a few questions before we get to the negotiations?"

"Maybe. Depends on what the questions are. If they are questions about my marriage, I will be happy to tell you that my husband was an adulterer who deserved to die. Any other questions?"

"How did you happen to meet Jack Habrowser, my student Hilary's ex-husband?"

A slow smile began to form on Marg's face. "That was easy. Hilary came on to my husband, as so many young women do. And my very weak and adulterous husband couldn't resist her charms. So I confronted her about it . . ." There was a ferocious gleam in her eyes as she looked over at Anna. "Did you know that for a while I even thought that *you* were having an affair with my husband?"

Anna shook her head and looked down at the table.

"Anyway, I told her to leave him alone. She said that if I ever came to her house again she would get a restraining order against me. Just as she had against her ex."

She paused for effect.

"I made contact with Jack. I'm very good with the Internet, you know. Entirely self-taught." She grinned. "Do you know you can learn all about how to make a bomb by going to the right place on the Web? That came in very handy."

The woman was truly insane.

Marg put her hands flat on the table. "I told Jack that Hilary was throwing herself unmercifully at my husband and asked him what he was going to do about it."

"Why should he do anything about it?" Anna asked.

Marg stared right into Anna's eyes. "Because a long time ago he was her husband. It's an unworthy husband who can't maintain control over his own wife."

Anna gave Marg a quizzical look, but kept her mouth shut.

"Jack e-mailed me. We met in Bangor. First thing he said was, 'What are we going to do about this?' And I said, 'I'd like to kill them both.' You know," she mused, "I wasn't really thinking of killing them until that precise moment. But that gave me the idea."

"So you and Jack planned all this," Anna said, keeping her voice even.

"I did it. I planned it all. Jack just went along with what I planned. He wanted to. I made him. Johnny deserved to die. He was immoral. My church even says so."

"Your church says it's okay to kill people?"

"God judges immoral people. He has through history and He does now and He will in the future."

Anna wanted more than anything to argue that point with Marg, but now was not the time.

Marg went on, "It was my plan, but I needed a person with muscle to help me carry it out. I worked it out perfectly. The mock disaster would be the perfect front." She paused and looked suddenly sad. "Except there were a few things I didn't count on."

"Like what?" Anna was interested.

"I didn't stop to think that the place would be crawling with EMTs and police. Also, the bomb went off ahead of time. That was Jack's fault. He detonated it too soon and that Claire girl wasn't supposed to die! I made Jack give me the phone. But I know you saw me when you went in. I saw you look over. . . ."

Anna nodded. "So that's why you tried to kill me and when that didn't work you framed me."

"I knew you had seen me and then when you came up to me in church and told me you knew everything, I figured you were asking for money."

"How was Lois involved in your plan?"

Marg laughed, a guttural sound. "She thinks she's such a good Christian lady, trying to help everybody. Befriended me just so she could show me some Christian charity." She spat out the words *Christian* and *charity*.

"Where is Jack now?"

Marg ignored Anna and pushed herself away from the table and stood up. "Now," she said. "How much money do you want to keep quiet?" Her back was to Anna when she said this and she was walking toward her kitchen sink. Anna stood, waited, watched her.

Anna said, “How much are you prepared to part with?”

“Look at this house. I’ll get everything when Johnny dies. Poor dear. And I don’t think he’s going to make it. I’m quite sure he’s not.”

When Marg turned back to face her, she was holding a small revolver and pointing it directly at Anna.

“Marg, put the gun down. Don’t shoot me. That will solve nothing.” Even though Anna spoke as clearly and as loudly as she could, she was trembling with fear.

At that instant, Anna heard a loud noise as the front door banged open and boots thudded down the hardwood floor.

“Police! This is the police!” Stu yelled as he ran toward the kitchen.

Marg didn’t drop her gun. Instead, she swung it wildly toward the noise and started firing. In the kitchen the sound of gunfire was deafening.

Anna dropped to the floor. She was under the table before the second shot was fired. She heard five loud shots and a lot of clicking. Had Marg shot Stu? Was Stu okay? Where was everybody?

From under the table, Anna heard Stu yell, “Police! Drop the gun, Marg!”

Marg was yelling and screaming at Stu. She was yelling and cursing at her gun as she continued to click away with the empty revolver. Anna could see Stu's legs and boots to the left.

She looked to the right and saw Marg's legs and feet, but her feet were not on the ground. Anna heard the gun hit the ceramic tile floor and saw it skid toward the refrigerator. Behind Marg's suspended feet Anna saw another set of legs and shoes. And then there were two people down at her level across the room.

"Marg Seeley, you are under arrest for the murder of Claire Sweeney and Hilary Jonas." It was Liz's loud voice. Marg was forced down on the floor. Liz had one knee on Marg's back, handcuffing her and attempting to read her her rights while the woman squirmed and yelled about how they would all rot in hell for what they were doing. God would surely judge them. They would all pay. Adulterers and immoral people would have their comeuppance.

While Liz was putting the cuffs on Marg, Stu gently helped Anna out from under the table. He sat her on a chair, gave her a quick hug and said, "Don't go anywhere."

Anna watched Stu pick up the little revolver with a pencil and put it in a plastic bag. It took Liz and Alec to carry Marg, kicking and screaming, to the waiting squad car.

Two officers from DeLorme had also appeared in the kitchen during the melee, and a woman officer was now gently removing the small transmitter and microphone that had been taped to Anna's chest. She no longer needed to wear these items. They had done their job. They had recorded it all. The officer said it gave them quite a start when they heard Anna say the word *gun*. The woman said she had done a super job and told Anna that anytime she wanted to come to DeLorme and work undercover, she was welcome to.

"That's not my cup of tea, I'm afraid," Anna said. She was still shaky from her ordeal. Even though she was the one who had proposed the idea of seeing Marg by herself.

"I can get her to talk to me," Anna had told them earlier. "She already thinks I know everything about her, that's why she freaked out so much when I spoke with her at her church. That's one of the things that made me know I was on the right track. When I told her that I knew everything, she thought I really did."

"Well, we got her," said one of the officers.

"And it will just be a matter of time before we find and pick up Jack Habrowser, her reluctant partner in crime."

Anna nodded. She was conscious of the way Stu leaned against the wall, looking at her. It seemed his gaze was fixed only on her. It made her nervous in a weird sort of way, and she couldn't help but remember the previous evening when he had kissed her.

Was she ready to trust someone again? What if after a week or a month, he took her face in his hands and told her that he wasn't really a Christian? That he never had been? Maybe he'd also say that he'd never loved her. That he'd just wanted to get to know her better, so he'd pretended. And that he found her goody-goody act quite charming. What if she ended up being afraid? She didn't think her heart could withstand another blow.

And yet, the way he was looking at her, the things he had told her. Peter had never been like that. Even when he'd accompanied her to church, he'd looked bored. She had been so starstruck that she had ignored these things. She had to believe that her experience in California had taught her something. And objectively Stu seemed real and genuine.

Stu approached her now, smiling in that shy way of his. He took her left hand in his and said, "We have to head down to the police station. And after that, I'll take you home." He played with her fingers as he said these words. "We need to tell your mother and your aunt how things went."

"I'm sure they've been praying the whole time," Anna said. "My mother didn't want me to do this."

Stu grinned. "She told me as much. How are you feeling about it all?"

"Okay, I guess. I'm feeling sad that Marg was so

desperate that she felt she had to do this. I'm just glad it's all over."

"Not quite," Stu said. "We still have to find Hilary's ex-husband."

They were walking to Stu's car, quite close together. The day was crisp, clear, and a few stray autumn leaves blew around their ankles. They lingered beside Stu's car. She knew they were expected at the police station, yet she wanted to stay within this moment for a while, the two of them standing so close together. Stu opened his mouth as if to say something, and then closed it again. Instead, he brought her to him and kissed her.

It had been a long time since Stu had allowed himself to feel this way about a woman. When Alesha died in that roadside bombing in Iraq, it was as if everything that made him feel anything had died, as well. And yet, as he held this woman's face in his hands as they stood beside his car, he began to realize something. Love is always about loss. But, if you don't allow yourself to be open to the possibility of loss, you don't open yourself to the possibility of love. And as he looked down into her eyes he realized that he was willing to try again. No matter what the future brought.

He kissed her again.

EPILOGUE

Stu and Anna were married three days after Christmas. They chose December 28 because with all the Christmas concerts and parties it was the only night that the little white church in Whisper Lake Crossing was free. Plus, they had the added bonus that the church was already decorated.

Anna's cast was removed just before Christmas, and the doctor seemed pleased with how her arm and hand had healed, especially since she could very easily have lost it. By her wedding day, she still only had limited use of her thumb and forefinger. But with hard work, exercise and physiotherapy twice a week, things were steadily improving. At least she could put her contact lenses in, apply makeup and blow-dry her hair without requiring help. That pleased her, but what she wanted to do most of all was to hold her wedding bouquet without dropping it. Sometimes her forefinger moved of its own accord.

On her wedding day she carried a white bouquet intermixed with holly berries. She managed to get all the way up the aisle without dropping it. She made it into the waiting arms of her handsome groom. Stu smiled as he watched Anna walk toward him. Stu was decked out in his most formal police attire.

Catherine and Lois were there, along with

Rodney and the rest of her students. The townspeople were there in abundance, which included Alec and Megan, Steve and Nori and their two daughters, Liz, Marlene and Roy, and Peach and Pete, the two elderly gentlemen who always hung out at the Schooner Café. It seemed as if the police from the other area departments were there, as well. After the wedding, everybody jammed into the Schooner Café for a wonderful reception.

Marg was charged with the murder of Hilary Jonas and Claire Sweeney. By Christmas she was still awaiting trial. It kept being put off, pending a definitive report on the status of her mental health. According to all reports gathered so far, she still ranted on and on about the judgment of God. A day after her arrest, Jack turned himself in.

Marg, the police learned, was entirely responsible for everything. She'd hunted down Jack Habrowser. She had found some small thing to blackmail him with, and orchestrated the whole show. Under her thumb, she forced him to dress in the green scrubs and terrify Anna in the hospital. He was also the one who pushed a cartload of pillows the day that Stu saw him. Marg learned online how to wire a switch so that the person touching it would get immediately shocked and possibly die. She and Jack jimmied the box the day Anna was in the hospital for her checkup. Marg also left her the notes and the text message.

She coerced Jack into stringing the wire on Stu's bike path. Marg also demanded that Jack follow Stu to see where he was going. Marg wanted to keep tabs on him.

Her plans, however, hadn't gone exactly as she hoped. The bomb wasn't supposed to be detonated until the following day. Marg planned the bomb to go off early in the morning when she knew her husband would be there and no one else. The bomb went off because Jack was trying to take the phone away from Marg. He wanted out of the whole scheme. The last thing he wanted to do was kill Hilary. He and Marg fought over that cell phone outside City Hall and the bomb she had made, following instructions she'd downloaded from the Internet, detonated.

Her court-appointed lawyer was arguing that Marg was severely emotionally and physically abused, and this caused her breakdown.

Lois, of course, felt terrible. All she was trying to do was help Marg, and she got caught up in the rhetoric of Marg's church. She had since done an about-face and now was active in the little white Whisper Lake Crossing Church.

Peter was discovered in Las Vegas, where he'd holed up with his latest supermodel. He'd had nothing to do with the bomb, as the video in the casino proved. He'd laughed off the "threatening" e-mail to Anna. It was meant as a joke, he'd said.

As for Brother Phil, as soon as the news broke

he moved his church on. No one knew where he was. No one really ever discovered who he was. Anna and Stu figured he'd gone on to infect another little town with his message of hatred and evil and judgment, not in the name of God, but in the name of religion.

Both Anna and Stu had come a long way since he'd dug her out of the rubble in front of City Hall. Through God's help he had learned to allow himself to feel again, eventually allowing himself to fall in love. Anna realized that despite the uncertainty of her injury, despite her horrific experience in California, God was molding her into the person that would be the best she could be. He had loved her, and had always loved her.

Dear Reader,

A couple of winters ago I fell on the ice and broke my right arm. I'm right-handed, and I'm a writer. It was quite a traumatic experience to be a writer and not even able to even make out my own shopping list.

Anna Barker, also right-handed, is an esthetician with hopes for a career in stage makeup. In the first chapter, however, her right hand is badly injured in a serious accident in which a couple of her students are killed. How will she work? Will she ever get the use of her hand back? Are all her dreams dashed? How does she manage with what is known as "survivor's guilt"?

Plus, with a recent shattered love experience, she didn't feel her life was worth a whole lot. She felt that all she was doing was "waiting," waiting on God, waiting for something to happen in her life, waiting for her arm to heal.

I wanted to explore all these feelings and thoughts when I set out to write *Critical Impact*, this third book in my Whisper Lake series.

If you have ever had to "wait" on God to meet some important need of yours, I would love to hear from you. My e-mail address is: Linda@writerhall.com.

I also would invite you to visit my Web site: writerhall.com.

Linda Hall

QUESTIONS FOR DISCUSSION

1. Have you ever lost the physical ability to do some important task? How did you manage? What did you learn from that experience?

2. What does it mean to "wait on the Lord"? What was Anna waiting for? Have you ever had to wait for God to answer a prayer? Was the answer you got the one you wanted? Why or why not?

3. Which character do you identify with the most, and why?

4. Lois saw Marg as a needy person who needed help. So she went to church with her and offered to be her friend. In your opinion, was this a wise thing? Why or why not?

5. Have you ever been in Lois's shoes—trying to help a needy person and yet having your efforts backfire? Explain.

6. What was the dangerous teaching in Brother Phil's church that Marg really took to heart?

7. Do you think Marg was justified in doing what she did? Why or why not? How does God's grace fit into this picture?

8. Stu's wife was killed in Iraq, and he vowed that he would never love anyone again. What was so different about Anna that he was drawn to her?

9. What would you have done if you had received the handwritten note telling you not to go to the police? Would you have gone to the police? Why or why not?

10. In the end, Anna finally realized that God loves her. In your opinion, what was that turning point?

Center Point Publishing
600 Brooks Road ● PO Box 1
Thorndike ME 04986-0001 USA

(207) 568-3717

US & Canada:
1 800 929-9108
www.centerpointlargeprint.com